MAN SPLAIN

ON A MANHUNT
BOOK 4

VANESSA VALE

Man Cave by Vanessa Vale

Cover design: Sarah Hansen/Okay Creations

Cover graphic: Deposit Photos: levchishinae

I'm a billionaire CEO. An expert fixer. I just found my next fix…

It's literally my job to make sure everything goes to plan. I'm really f-ing good at it.

But when the beautiful coffee shop owner refuses a corporate loan to keep her business afloat solely because we had a slightly-drunk quickie, it makes me crazy.

Insane. Frustrated. Turned on. Especially when I discover the stubborn woman chooses instead to be a cam girl to pay her bills. Of course, I step in, because:

1. I need to make this right.
2. There's no way another man is going to glimpse one gorgeous inch of her.
3. It's my fault.

I buy up all her cam time. Problem solved.

Except this is a plan I didn't think through. Eve doesn't know she's falling for the same guy on and off the screen.

What happens when she learns the truth?

All I know is this may be the one problem I can't fix.

With all the books in the On A Manhunt series, it's always open season on men.

1

EVE

OWNING a coffee shop meant early mornings. I was used to it. Used to waking up in the dark and going to bed when some finished their dinner. The past two days, the second my alarm blared, I was up, wide awake and eager.

Eager like a beaver.

Or my *beaver* was eager.

Why?

My very attractive, very bare neighbor.

Bare, as in bare ass. And bare *front*.

The naked guy in the house behind mine was a new morning addition. I'd never seen him before, dressed or undressed. Or maybe the person who lived there before didn't get up this early. Or walked around without clothes–and no blinds–with the light on.

Or maybe it was the leaves on the trees that usually blocked the view into that backyard which were now gone for the winter. Or that...

Who cared? I didn't.

All I knew was that Michelangelo's David had nothing on this guy. He was hung. And ripped. And made me horny at five in the morning.

No one was horny at that time of day.

Jumping from bed, I kept my lights off and padded over to my bedroom window, slid the curtain back and–

YES!

Mr. Big Dick was up! The man himself, I meant. And his Big Dick. Yes, it was impressive enough to be capitalized.

He was on the phone, like he had been the previous times. The first morning, I opened my curtain and saw him. Blinked. Rubbed my eyes because... what!? A naked man?

Then I ogled. Drooled some, too.

He was there yesterday, too. Same thing. I kept the lights off so he didn't know I watched.

Me and my libido hoped he'd be back at it again this morning. And he was.

Female fist pump!

I watched as he strolled from the hallway to the

kitchen sink to the coffee maker back to the hallway, then into the bedroom as he talked on the phone. God bless the remodelers installing large windows on the back side of that house.

The guy was a pacer when he took a call.

And amazingly naked. Like toddlers who never liked to get dressed. But he was no toddler. Gah!

Did I mention he was also blond... everywhere. What was it about the drapes and curtains matching? They matched. Oh, they totally matched. Plus, a beard. Yum.

It was November. Wasn't he cold? It was hovering around freezing and it definitely didn't reflect in the junk hanging between his sturdy thighs. Guys–at least this one–definitely woke up with morning wood.

I sighed, rubbed my thighs together and wished there weren't two backyards between us. But I couldn't knock on the door and tell him I was a Peeping Tom and that I wanted to check out the merchandise up close. I couldn't drop by at five a.m. for some sugar and tell him to keep standing by the back door so I could see his eye color from my bedroom window. Although my eyesight wasn't *that* good.

No. If this scenario was reversed and he watched me, he'd be arrested. But there were no curtains on those windows. Or he didn't close the blinds. He was *asking* to be ogled and I owed it to women to do that ogling. Hell, that body *deserved* it.

This guy was my morning wake up secret. My fantasy where I imagined he knew exactly what to do with a woman. He wouldn't be gentle. Hell, no. Mr. Big Dick would be bold. A little dominant. Alpha... yeah, he'd go all Alpha on me and ensure I didn't walk right for a couple days. Oh, he'd fuck me not just once, but twice–or maybe three times–because he had the stamina to go again and again.

What did my friends always say? Dick was better than caffeine any day. Since I owned a coffee shop and had a shitty ex, I usually didn't agree. But now? Salivating over my mystery neighbor?

I was Team Morning Dick.

All. The. Way.

SILAS

"No, those figures don't match. There needs to be a ten percent increase."

I paced the short hallway, rubbing the back of my neck. I hated these early morning calls with Geneva, but with the time difference, if I waited until the start of my day in Denver–or in Hunter Valley where I was now–the Hyport staff would be ending theirs. There would be no way to get any work done on the merger if they were putting on their coats to go home.

I had similar calls in the evenings with Asia and the hotels there.

It was my life lately. As CEO of an international

company trying to close the biggest deal in decades–buying the Hyport Hotel conglomerate and merging all their hotels worldwide under James Hotel–I worked all the time. I was getting tired of the grind and ready for the papers to be signed. The never-ending meetings. Travel. Problems. The early mornings. Late nights.

One perk of these calls was that I didn't need to be at a desk. Or dressed. No one on the group call knew I was freeballing before dawn while waiting for my coffee to brew. I'd only stayed in this house in Hunter Valley a few times and it had become mine by default. Dex had used it first until he fell for Lindy. Then it was Theo's before he shacked up with Mallory.

Now, the only single James brother left, it was mine.

I slept naked, so when my cell rang, I climbed from bed and skipped boxers or sweats. I didn't need a suit or tie. I was alone in the house. Although, if I had a woman with me, I still wouldn't be dressed. One hadn't crossed my path, or been near my dick, in a while. Unlike all my brothers who'd pretty much become pussy whipped one after the other for amazing women. All in this small, Montana town. Maybe it was the water.

"Good," I added. "Keep me posted on the changes. Yes, I'll be flying out tomorrow, but we've been working on this for weeks. I need the regional plan modifications to me in advance of the meeting."

I hung up, grabbed a mug from the cabinet and filled it to the brim. The first sip perked me right up. The one thing I loved about Hunter Valley was the coffee. My older brother Mav found an amazing shop on Main Street where he got ground beans for all our houses. He'd also made a deal with the coffee shop owner to supply the James Inn when it opened.

I'd have to get into the coffee shop one of these days, if I ever stayed in town long enough. Maybe get a pink t-shirt of my own. Mav wore his a little too proudly for a fucker of his size.

Scrolling through my inbox on my laptop, I found my assistant's email with my day's agenda.

- *5 am - Call with Geneva*
- *James Inn - Hunter Valley - Mav and IT Techs*
- *Calls at 2:30, 3, 4:15 and 5 - Topics and agendas listed below*
- *Dinner at 6 with Mav and Theo - Address below*
- *10:15 pm - Call with Singapore Hyport reps*

Something soft and furry circled around my legs and scared the shit out of me.

Startled, I flung my coffee and it went everywhere, including all over me. "Fuck!"

Something shot across the floor followed by a weird

flip-flap sound. Covered in hot coffee, I stood there, stunned. That was an animal. Holy fuck. What the hell was it doing in the house? Dripping with cooling coffee, I went around the counter and into the laundry room where I thought the sound came from and flipped on the light. There, low to the floor, was a tiny dog door.

"What the hell?"

Grabbing a towel off the dryer, I wiped myself down as I went for my phone.

Standing in the kitchen, I dialed Theo.

"Do you have a *cat*?" I asked, the second he answered.

"What?" he said, his voice deep and rough with sleep. "Silas? Are you drunk?"

"No," I said, wiping down my right arm. "There was an animal in here that just rubbed up against my legs. Scared the shit out of me. It ran off."

"The cat came in the house?" He was more awake now.

"*Something* came inside. Jesus, it could have been a raccoon for all I know."

"There's a stray. Cat, not raccoon. I was feeding it and it got friendly enough to come up onto the porch. I had a dog door installed thinking it might come inside."

"It?"

"I haven't gotten close enough to find out if it's a boy or a girl."

I squatted down, used the towel to wipe the kitchen floor.

"I did, but I doubt it's coming back. Am I supposed to feed it or something?"

"I pay the neighbor kid to put some food in a bowl on the front stoop."

I hadn't noticed the bowl or a kid.

"If it's a stray, why give it a cat door? I mean, it lives outside."

"If you haven't noticed, it's fucking freezing. I thought it might want to come in."

I had no idea what had happened to my brother. Only a few months ago, he pretty much lived inside a hospital. No pets, no girlfriend, nothing but a surgical rotation and on-call status. Now he was worried about a stray cat staying warm.

"I'm all for saving a cat but give a guy some notice that a feral one may be my roommate. I almost burned my dick."

"I don't want to know what that means." He hung up.

Flinging the dirty towel back onto the laundry room floor, I refilled my mug and carried it into the bathroom. Turned on the shower. I was on-site all day with Mav at the inn, working to resolve the issue of tying the reservation systems together on the back end with the main James Corp hotels. Mav was tackling the boutique inn silo he'd built, and I took care of every other silo of the company. If silos were like balls that I had to juggle, it was like I was in charge of a ball pit at a kid's party center. With the possible purchase of the Hyport chain, my workload was crazier than usual. We were close to finishing the deal. I hoped only a few more weeks.

I sighed, stepping beneath the hot spray.

Theo was tucked into bed with Mal down the street. Mav with Bridget up in the foothills in that big monstrosity of a house. Dex and Lindy in his apartment in Denver. Me? I was in a different bed practically every day. My apartment in Denver, here in Hunter Valley, and hotels all over the world. This insanity, while self-induced, had to end soon. I was burnt out. I was lonely.

I envied how my brothers had all settled down. Mav had a dog. And Theo appeared to have a semi-feral cat. This deal had to go through. I had to redeem the James Hotel name with the Hyports after my father's past fiascos with them.

It was my company now and I wanted everyone to know I wasn't my father. The James Hotel was no longer under his control—since he was dead and buried—and I was taking the company in the right direction. Doubling the size was one way to do that.

But right now, I had too much work. Too much responsibility. Too much travel. A fling would be good. Or just a fuck. I gripped my dick and gave it a hard pull.

My hand was definitely *not* a willing, wet woman, but it would take the edge off.

Tonight I was having dinner with Mav and Theo, kicking back with some good food and a few drinks before I flew eight time zones for more negotiations.

Again.

3

EVE

I saw the name on my cell as it rang. Then again. "Hello, Father."

At two-thirty, it was between busy times, so I answered instead of letting it go to voicemail. He'd call again, so it was better to get it over with. For a second I wondered if he chose this quiet time intentionally, but quickly remembered he didn't do anything out of courtesy. It was just when he thought of me.

The Swing Band music I had playing wasn't too loud to bother the call—or customers.

"How are things downtown?" he asked, his voice as stiff and proper as someone who had a stick up his ass could be.

Downtown. As if he wasn't ten miles away up by the ski resort.

"*Things* are fine," I replied.

While he was a local himself, born and bred, he didn't do the quaint Main Street that made Hunter Valley unique.

It was below him to leave the posh area up by the resort. The one his parents founded. *Whatever.*

It wasn't below me. Never was.

"Yes. The lifts might start a week early," he replied. "How's your little shop?"

I rolled my eyes and grabbed a new bag of coffee beans from the display and gave it a squeeze, envisioning it was my father's neck.

"The *little* shop is doing well," I replied. "It is only ten miles from home. You can come down and see for yourself."

"Evelyn," he chided, using my name in that tone that was meant to shame. It used to work, the disappointment I felt in any decisions that didn't match theirs, but no longer.

"I've connected with a local inn to exclusively sell my beans for their restaurant, the small café, and placement in the rooms with the coffee makers." That should make him happier, telling him of the growth of Steaming Hotties. It was a big contract.

While I'd been friends with Bridget for a long time, it

was her boyfriend who I'd proposed the business arrangement to a few months ago. Maverick James, of the mega-big James Hotel chain family, was building a high-end inn in the area and stopped in frequently for coffee. I thought I had a little bit of a role in the two of them getting together, Bridge having spilled coffee all over the guy when they first met. Right here in the shop.

The *little shop* that my parents thought was me amusing myself before I settled down with Cheney Douglas.

My boyfriend since senior year of high school.

The one who our parents matched together.

The one who I was expected to marry, my fate decided–by them–when I was seventeen.

The one who I dumped a year ago when I realized– yeah, my head had been really far up my ass–he expected me to play with my coffee shop for a little while and amuse myself before returning to the resort side of town and become his stay-at-home wife.

The one who also kept pestering me about *when* my play time was going to end.

The one my father was going to mention in about thirty seconds.

That Cheney Douglas. I had no idea why he wanted to marry a woman who didn't like him.

Oh yeah. Money. I had lots of it. I was a Hunter, after

all. Yeah, Hunter, as in Hunter Valley. To my parents, I was the wild child, although not really wild. I just liked to wear dangling earrings. Cowboy boots. Jeans with rips in them.

Yeah, totally wild. Not a pearl earring or matching sweater set in sight.

"Ah yes, your magical beans."

If smoke could really come out of my ears, the fire alarm would be going off right now.

"Yes, most people think they're magical when they drink their first cup every morning," I countered. As if I was peddling something like magical mushrooms instead of the brew he had two cups of every morning.

"As I've told you before, you need to ensure that you–"

"Do not start mansplaining how to run a business when you are not employed," I snapped. He might be a Hunter by birth, but he didn't work for the resort. He didn't work, period.

He tsked me. "Evelyn, I–"

He was cut off with a rustle and the sound of a phone scuffle.

"Evelyn, dear." My mother stole the phone away. I wasn't sure if it was to keep the peace or because she couldn't wait a second longer to meddle herself. I could see her in her dress, either in pink or pale blue, with her grandmother's pearls about her neck. "I spoke to

Cheney's mother and she said Cheney hasn't heard from you."

Definitely to meddle.

"That's because we're not together," I reminded. "I have no reason–or interest–to talk to him."

"Does he know that?"

"I feel confident that my ex knows he's an ex," I grumbled. I'd told him face-to-face. In voicemails. Texts. Again face-to-face.

"Well, you'll see him in a few weeks at the party at the club. I'm sure you'll make things right before then."

"What party?" I skipped the part about why I needed to make things right. I thought that him being my ex was completely right.

"The annual holiday party," she said, although she probably wanted to add a *duh* onto the end. "You're coming, of course. I have a dress for you. Velvet and without all the patterns and layering you find in the bargain basement for these days. With your business closing, I didn't think you'd have time to find one."

The bell above the door dinged and I turned and waved at a customer.

I skipped over the fact that my mother took another dig at my wardrobe for the important gem. "My business closing?"

"Cheney told me the other day at the club that you're shutting your coffee shop down. Your father said it was just a phase and I can see now that he was right. Letting you use some of your trust fund to play coffee shop was money well spent and now we can plan your wedding!"

"What?" I asked.

I usually kept my voice calm with my parents. Any shift in my tone was something they pounced on. I was too emotional. Too dramatic. Making too much out of nothing. They were exceptional at gaslighting, using my anger and frustration with them as proof I was unrealistic with my life choices. I took a deep breath.

"I'm not going through a *phase* and my coffee shop isn't closing. I'm not *playing* at anything. I live in a cute little house downtown. Just because my clothes aren't made with cashmere doesn't mean they are castoffs. Why would I move back in with you? Why would you want me to?"

"Evelyn–"

"I have a customer. I have to go."

"But–"

I hung up, wishing I could put something stronger than non-dairy milk into a cup of coffee. I pasted a smile on my face for the customer and got back to work. To my business that was *not* closing.

I spent long enough being controlled and my life planned by others. I was done with that. I'd majored in business in college instead of French like my mother wanted. My father had been pleased with my choice, saying I might get a role in running the Hunter Valley Resort. Not *his* business because he didn't do anything with the company except spend the profits. It had been his parents who built it from scratch and made it a success. Not just his father, but his mother as well. She'd been the skier. The sporty one who saw the potential for turning the local mountains into a winter destination. Between my grandfather's business sense and my grandmother's vision, they made it what it was today. They'd made the place, the entire town, enduring. Just like their love for each other.

Like coffee. Everyone always needed coffee. I'd done my senior project on the business plan for Steaming Hotties, and I'd made it happen after graduation. Not for *fun*. Not shits and giggles or a phase or whatever else my parents and Cheney thought. This place was *my* shop. My baby. My business. My livelihood.

Nothing was going to change that. Not Cheney. Not my parents.

4

SILAS

Mᴀᴠ ᴀɴᴅ Tʜᴇᴏ bailed on me. When we were at the inn, Mav mentioned that Bridge had a make-up day Physics Fair at school where they dropped specially designed egg protectors off the roof to see if their precious cargo could keep from cracking. Since it had snowed the past few days and today was warmer and dry, it was happening. What Mav had to do with the event, I had no idea. But whatever Bridge needed, Bridge got. He was whipped. Hard core.

As for Theo, he'd been pulled into some kind of medical training with the fire department. So I didn't feel abandoned, he'd invited me to participate, saying they were looking for volunteers for IV stick practice.

No fucking way. I asked him if Mallory had offered her veins and she'd said no fucking way as well.

So my last night in Hunter Valley was solo. I was at the bar nursing a beer. I'd put in an order for a burger, but it hadn't been dropped off yet. For now, I was working my way through a bowl of baby pretzels.

Someone slid up to the bar beside me. I picked up a hint of coffee and... citrus. "Hey, can I get a glass of your house white?" the woman asked the bartender.

She shifted, then looked my way. Her eyes widened as if she saw a ghost.

"Holy shit," she whispered, eyeing me. Then eyeing me some more. Her gaze raked down my body in hot perusal. Like she knew what I looked like naked. Or wanted to.

I offered her a small smile, enjoying her heated and *complete* study. Not from *this* woman. Hell, no. She could look all she wanted.

And touch, too.

"I don't think I've seen anyone look something over quite so thoroughly since the cattle auction at the county fair back in July," I murmured.

She blushed and that sure as hell looked pretty on her. It was completely opposite of how she looked at me just seconds before. Sultry and sweet. Quite the combo.

"Oh, um," she said, glancing away. "Sorry. I... um, I thought you looked familiar."

She didn't look familiar to me. I'd have totally remembered her. Clothed, naked, there would be no forgetting. No fucking way. She was stunning.

While she was flustered, I took my time studying her in return. Gray eyes fringed with dark lashes, pert nose, full lips. Her skin was pale and flawless, except for a little freckle or mole by the corner of her right eye. Long, dark hair framed her narrow face. Silver earrings dangled from her ears. She wore a blue dress that hit right at the knee beneath a plum-colored fleece coat. She must have just come in. With the jacket unzipped, I couldn't miss her perfect handful-sized breasts, ones my palms itched to cup. Neither could I miss the rest of her curves, and there were plenty. And fuck me, to complete the casual outfit, she wore western boots.

She looked absolutely nothing like the corporate women I met at the various James Corp offices or hotels around the world. I doubted any of them owned boots like those. Instantly, I imagined her wearing them and nothing else.

I liked what I saw. I liked it a lot. The way she'd literally fucked me with her eyes, it was clear she was into me. It didn't feel like a pick up, but more like seeing me was a shock. As if she saw me and BAM. Hit by the hots.

When I finished a thorough onceover of my own and met her gaze again, I felt it. Sizzle. Heat. The way she squirmed wasn't from embarrassment. It was need.

My dick perked up because... hell yeah. Sitting was becoming really fucking uncomfortable.

She cleared her throat and looked away first. "County fair? You were never in 4H," she said and her lip quirked.

I put my hand on my chest. "Is it because I'm not wearing a snap shirt?"

I didn't own a snap shirt, but I'd buy a bunch of them if it was her thing.

Her eyes widened in mock surprise. "Total stereo-type. You don't have to be a cowboy to wear a snap shirt. You just have to–"

"—want to get your shirt off quickly?" I finished, smiling fully now.

She grinned. "Exactly." Her gaze lowered to my chest, and I had to wonder if she was wishing I had on a snap shirt so she could tug it open. The shirt I wore had buttons and I'd sacrifice every one if she wanted to yank at it.

The bartender slid a glass of wine toward her and she looked his way. "Thank you."

"On me," I told him. He nodded, then went to help someone else.

"Join me?" I asked, tipping my head to the empty stool beside mine. Flirting with a woman was better than hanging with my loser brothers. And she was a fuck-ton prettier. "Unless you're here with someone." I glanced around, looking for whomever she might be with, then leaned close. "Although the way you were checking me out, I'm guessing that's a no."

She tucked her hair back and she blushed some more. "No, I mean, yes... I came in alone. And yeah, sorry about that."

"Don't be. Nothing wrong with seeing something you like."

She'd started this whole thing with her imagining what I looked like without clothes. I was just pushing things along. If she wanted to see me naked... perhaps as much as I wanted to see every perfect inch of her, I was all for it. I took another moment to take her in from top to bottom as if taking inventory.

"I *really* like what I see right back. Join me," I repeated.

Her eyes met mine. Held. What was it about her? About those eyes? Why was I flirting with a woman at a bar? I didn't do that. Especially when I wasn't at home. Oh yeah, stood up by my brothers. I was too old for random hookups, but there was something different about her that called to me. Or maybe I was just tired of fucking my hand.

"Okay," she whispered, maybe to herself. She dropped onto the stool beside me.

"I'm Silas. I'm not a cowboy and I've never been in 4H. I really did go to the county fair in July though."

She took a sip of her wine and studied me. "Eve."

"What brings you in for a drink, Eve?"

She frowned at her glass of wine as if it had done her wrong. "Overbearing family. You?"

"Mine ditched me for falling eggs and bloodletting."

She frowned. "I'm not sure if I want to know what that means. Should I be freaked out or intrigued?"

I laughed. "Intrigued, although my brothers are not all that exciting. And it means they have weird priorities." I signaled the bartender, then looked at Eve. Fuck her eyes were now a slate blue. How did they switch colors like that? "Talking about families calls for something stronger. You like tequila?"

This was where she could turn me down. Say no thanks and savor her glass of wine. But she didn't. Instead, she was all in. "As long as there's a lot of lime."

"Two shots of tequila with lots of lime," I told the bartender.

A minute later, we held up our shots. "What should we toast?" I asked.

She looked to me with those sparkling gray eyes, thought for a moment. "Anything but family."

I met her gaze, then let it rove over her pretty face. "To liking what we see."

5

SILAS

Two hours of flirting and a few more shots of tequila later, I led Eve down the dim hallway with her small hand in mine. The music and other bar patrons were left behind. I passed the restrooms. No way was I fucking a woman in a bathroom stall. My dick might be hard for the upcoming quickie, but I had some standards.

I tried the handle on the next door. Locked. I went to the last one, twisted the knob. It opened and I pulled her inside.

She giggled, a sign we were both a little drunk. A *little*. Buzzed. Enough to let our inhibitions down but not too much where we'd have hangovers and regrets in the morning.

I reached out, flicked a light switch. Perfect. An office. I turned us around and pressed her into the door. Her eyes widened, and so did her smile, when it clicked shut behind her.

"You still want this?" I asked, stroking her soft cheek. Her dark hair brushed her shoulder and I tucked it back. It was one thing to sit at a bar and talk about fucking each other, it was another for me to sink balls deep in a back office without getting more than her name.

When you squirm on your stool like that, I have to wonder if your pussy's achy.

God, what is it about you? I need... I–

You need to come?

Yes.

I'll make you come. How do you want it? Dick? Mouth?

Dick. I definitely want that dick.

I'd never forget that sentence as long as I lived. *I definitely want that dick.*

As if she knew it personally.

I hopped off my stool and tugged her down the hall.

Now, closed in this back office together, I waited for confirmation she was still all in.

I wanted her, but I wasn't an asshole.

She bit her lip for a second as her gaze raked over me, then nodded. Her hands went to the back of my neck to tug me down–since I was at least six inches taller. "Kiss me."

I did. Fuck, yes.

I sank into the kiss. Into her. My hands roamed, felt her soft curves beneath her dress.

When my lips grazed her jaw and down her neck, she was panting and her hands moved to my belt. She was an aggressive little thing. Needy.

"You wet?" I asked, holding still as she pushed my jeans low on my hips, reaching in and taking a firm grip on my dick.

"I knew it," she said, but I was too far gone to wonder *what* she knew. That I was big? That I was hard for her? That–

"Fuck," I muttered, my eyes falling closed, when she gave it a good, hard pump.

"I'm wet," she answered finally.

I blinked, took in her aroused gaze. The plump, kiss-swollen lips. "Show me."

Unfortunately, she had to let go of me to pull up her flirty dress, the one that had ridden up her thigh every time she shifted in her barstool earlier.

This woman wasn't shy. When her pink panties were revealed, she slipped two fingers beneath the gusset and sunk them deep.

"Fuck, Eve." Pre-cum seeped from the tip of my dick. I wanted to replace those fingers right fucking now. That had me pulling out my wallet and grabbing a condom.

The only way this was moving forward was if I was wrapped.

She held her fingers up. "See?" The tips were glistening. I grabbed her wrist and licked the wetness off.

"So fucking sweet."

Her eyes widened and when I let her go, she spun about, pressed her hands into the door, ass canted out. "Hurry."

Holy. Fucking. Shit. Needy and gorgeous.

I shook my head, grabbed her about the waist and spun us both so she was bent over the desk. I didn't know who owned the place, but I probably owed him a new workspace after this.

I pushed the hem of her dress up and over her back, then instead of sliding those pretty panties down, I ripped them right off and tucked them in my pocket.

"Widen those feet. Let me see your pussy," I ordered as I rolled the condom down my length. I was throbbing with the need to fuck.

It had been a while and never quite like this.

She glanced over her shoulder past me and to the closed door.

"You worried someone might find us?" I asked. It was a distinct possibility. I didn't lock the door.

She whimpered but didn't look the least bit afraid. In fact, she seemed to like the idea of being caught.

Me? If someone wanted to see my bare butt as I

fucked, I didn't care.

Palming one pale globe of her perfect ass, I caressed that soft skin. Then gave it a quick, light spank. "You're a dirty girl, aren't you? Bent over a desk and ready to be fucked." I cupped her pussy and felt how wet and ready she was. "So needy for my dick that you don't care who might see."

The words might have been degrading. But not now. Not with her. It was fact. And it was fucking hot. She was a sexual dream come true.

She wiggled her hips, thrust her butt up further. "Hurry," she said again.

Hurry? No fucking problem. I stepped close, lined up and since I knew she was wet and ready, plunged deep.

"Fuck!" I practically shouted as her inner walls clenched and rippled, adjusting to being crammed full. Holy shit, she felt so fucking good. My fingers clenched on her hips, her ass a soft cushion as I slapped against her.

"Yes," she hissed. Resting on her forearms, she dropped her head between them. "God, I needed this."

"You need this? Fuck, my dick loves your pussy," I said, pulling back then filling her once again. Fuck, she was heaven. And I sure as shit needed this, too.

"Don't be gentle," she said, glancing back at me and giving me those dark, needy eyes.

"Sweetheart, I couldn't be gentle if I tried."

6

EVE

I WAS bent over a desk in the bar's back office getting fucked. Railed. Totally railed. This *so* wasn't me, but I liked it. No, liked wasn't the right word.

Loved it.

Craved it. I'd never had it like this before.

Needed it.

Oh, did I need it.

Even if I didn't know if he'd flipped the lock on the doorknob and chanced anyone walking in at any time. The idea of being caught made it hotter.

I was having sex with my neighbor, Mr. Big Dick. The way he was gripping my hips and fucking me from behind, I wasn't doing all that much except rolling my butt up to try and meet his hard thrusts. He was fucking me. Controlling me. Dominating.

And he lived up to his name and to what I glimpsed across our backyards. He really *was* big. I didn't need to go to my eye doctor for a while. I could spot a Big Dick at forty feet without glasses.

Now? It hit me nice and deep. Hard.

I gripped the edge of the desk in front of me, held on.

"Can you come like this?" he asked, his voice deep. Ragged.

I stared at the wall in front of me and tried to keep my moaning as quiet as possible.

"I need... clit."

He pulled all the way out. "No!" I cried. "What are you–"

I turned my head, upset because he'd stopped fucking me. For a second I wondered if he didn't like the idea of having to work my clit and gave up, but he dropped to his knees and put his mouth on me.

From behind.

"Oh my God!" I practically screamed. I was so worked up from him fucking me that the little flicks of his tongue on my clit were intense. I went up on my toes as he gripped the backs of my thighs and held me wide open. He was diligent. Focused. Ruthlessly precise, as if me coming was the top of his to-do list. Maybe the only thing on it. "Oh please!"

I came... because... he was a fucking sex god.

It was possible the office door opened and I heard a "Sorry" before it was shut again, but I also heard angels and harps and Silas telling me I was a good girl for coming all over his face.

Before I recovered, he was up and in me again. Deep.

He set a hand on the hard surface by my head and loomed. "That was one," he murmured, leaning close.

"Did someone come in?" I asked, his hips rolling in this magical way that had me whimpering and on the brink of coming all over again. I wasn't sure if I should be mortified or proud.

"Maybe. I was too busy with a face full of pussy to notice."

I turned my head and he kissed my jaw, my neck. "Give me another," he ordered, as if telling people what to do came natural to him. "This time you'll milk my dick when you do."

He pushed off, pulled my hip so I slid backward on the desk giving him room to reach beneath me and... oh shit. I had no choice to obey because OH MY GOD.

He found my clit with his fingers. One try. No map. Although he'd already been up close and friendly with it with his tongue. "Yes!" I cried, rolling my hips trying to reach for that orgasm.

His free hand slid, down over my butt, caressing, then between–

"Holy—YESSSSS!"

He put his thumb on my butt...well, not butt. *There.* I'd never had a guy touch me in that place before. Cheney wouldn't have been caught dead in that region. He wouldn't do doggy-style over a desk either. Or in the back of a bar.

I didn't know I could be this wet. This aroused. That I could come twice.

Who knew that spot was an orgasm button? One brush with his thumb and I literally detonated like a bomb.

Which set him off. I felt him swell, then hold himself deep as he made this growly-groan sound and came.

That had been... it was... no words.

Silas might be a quickie and that was fine. I always knew Cheney wasn't a porn star in the sack, but there was no way–even if I'd lost my mind–I'd ever go back to Mr. Boring Dick. If you're going to get over one guy you need to get under another, right? RIGHT. Abso-fucking-lutely.

7

SILAS

"The meeting is at ten in the general manager's office on the third floor. I sent you an agenda of talking points about the merging of employees," Bradley said. I had him on a video call, but I couldn't see his face since I was looking at a different window on my laptop scanning the agenda I'd opened from his email. "Do you need me to give you bios on each of the Hyport leadership who will be there?"

"No."

"After, a car will take you to lunch with the owner of the boutique hotel in Frederikshavn. She's made the trip down from the north to meet you."

He pronounced the town completely differently than

how it looked written in my travel itinerary. I didn't speak Danish, but it sounded like Bradley did.

"Name?"

He shared her name and a brief bio.

"After?"

"Airport. Flight back to Denver. Then you have three hours of meetings, meet-and-greets and—"

"Send that info to me tomorrow and I'll go over it on the plane."

"Will do."

My cell rang and I grabbed it from the side table. "It's Dex," I said.

"Tell him good game yesterday. Two goals and an assist."

I'd worked with Bradley long enough to know he was sharing the stats, like the amazing assistant he was, so I could praise my brother regardless that I'd missed the game.

"Thanks, Bradley."

The video call ended and I swiped my cell.

"Where the hell are you?" Dex asked right away.

"Denmark." I slapped my laptop closed. A quick glance out the hotel room window offered nothing but inky black. This far north, it was dark early this time of year. It didn't matter to me because my internal clock had no idea what time it was. All I knew was that I wasn't tired, which meant jet lag was fucking with me. What else was new?

Since the summer, Mav was content with the James Inn projects and nothing more. He hadn't stepped foot in the Denver corporate office in three months. He wasn't involved in this Hyport sale. Theo and Dex never had a hand in the business. That left me to carry on James Corp, to run the family hotel business. And grow it, the latest step of that with the Hyport deal. That meant travel. That meant being a better juggler than a clown at the circus.

"Jesus. You travel more than I do," Dex pointed out. "Is this all for that merger?"

That was saying a lot since my not-so-little brother was a professional hockey player and pretty much on the road eight months out of the year. But he stayed mostly in North America. Me? Lately, I was on every continent but.

"Yeah."

"That's the deal that Dad fucked up, right?"

I sighed. "Yes. He slept with the owner's personal assistant. Among other things."

"Figures," Dex said on a grunt. We both knew how much of a philanderer and total dickhead our father was. He fucked anything that wore a skirt. The younger the better. He hadn't cared if his actions were far from ethical or completely immoral and totally inappropriate.

Not only had he slept with that assistant, he took his merger team and a few from Hyport Asia to a brothel in Thailand. The place had specialized in barely legal women. Yeah, that kind of not-safe-for-work shenanigans.

The deal hadn't gone through, obviously, and the Hyport team had wanted nothing to do with James Corp. Until me. Until I'd buried my father's antics right along with him.

"How long are you there?"

"Meetings are done for today. I have things in the morning, then I'm headed back to Denver. For a day. Then I go to Singapore to meet the Hyport Asia division."

It was tempting for me to head up to Hunter Valley when I got to Denver. A quick flight to Montana and I could see Eve again. Pick up where we left off.

"Why not go the other way straight to Singapore? It'd be a lot faster."

"Taking up geography in your free time?" I stood and went to the tray of coffee and spandauer that had been brought to me when I returned to my room. I grabbed one of the pastries laced with cinnamon—my favorite one and always asked for it when I stayed here—and took a bite.

Fuck, they were good. Even if it was late at night.

He laughed. "I'm spending all my free time balls deep in my woman trying to knock her up."

I didn't really need to picture Dex and Lindy going at it, but Dex had always been an oversharer. Now that he was getting some on the regular, and with the woman he was keeping... hell, he'd married her, he was being an asshole about it. Or he didn't really think about the fact that I was the only brother left who wasn't having sex. Okay, once and in the back room of a bar. A spectacular, desk-sex quickie.

Dex wanted babies and a picket fence with Lindy and they weren't wasting any time making that happen. I figured he had a few years left with the Silvermines, then he'd settle down in Hunter Valley and be a peewee hockey coach for the rest of his life.

"You need to find yourself one."

I frowned. "I hope you only mean sex because I have no intention of knocking any woman up," I said, my mouth full. No way. I was all for kids, but I didn't want a Baby Mama. But sex? Oh, I'd go back for round two with Eve. My dick twitched at the thought.

"What the hell are you eating?"

"A Danish." I stared at the sugary snack. I skipped the coffee because caffeine was the last thing I needed. Although I probably didn't need a sugar rush either. I'd sleep on the plane. After I went through the latest itinerary, agenda, contract, or whatever else Bradley sent to me to review. "Although in Denmark they're not called Danishes. Go figure."

"I thought it was night there."

"It is."

"Back to making babies. You don't have to pull the goalie. Just show up for practice."

I rolled my eyes. "You and your hockey analogies."

"Your dick isn't meant for *just* procreating. You can whip it out and fuck with it every once in a while."

"I did." I said, shoving the last piece of spandauer in my mouth.

"This year?"

I sighed, flopped down on a reading chair by the window that overlooked Copenhagen. With sugary fingers I worked open the top button on my shirt and loosened my tie. I didn't want to wonder why my brother thought I hadn't had sex at any time this year.

"Before I left."

"You were in Hunter Valley then." He paused, clearly processing. "Wait. Wait... who the hell did you sleep with in Hunter Valley?"

"One-night stand." I pictured Eve, bent over that desk with her dress flipped up, cowboy boots on, and that peach of an ass all perfect and... fuck. Now I was hard. And getting harder as I thought of how her pussy felt clamping down on my dick as she came. How she'd tasted when I'd eaten her out mid-fuck. The sound of her whimpers and moans of pleasure... she was a fucking siren.

He whistled. "So you're not going to see her again."

I ran my hand down my face, felt a few crumbs fall. "We fucked. She thanked me. She walked out practically before I got the condom off."

"That's it?"

"Are you expecting me to send you an engraved invitation to our wedding? We had a few drinks and things got... hot."

Hot? She'd been scorching. Right there with me. Bold. Kinky, or at least a little bit. She had a touch of voyeur in her. Someone *had* opened the door and caught us. I'd had my mouth on her slick pussy, feeling her orgasm on my tongue. The entire pro ski team could have come in and supervised and I wouldn't have cared.

She'd liked being beneath me. *Really* liked my dick. She'd gotten off on the possibility of being caught. Twice.

Then she thanked me and left.

Wham, bam, thank you, sir.

"Yeah, but you could have coaxed her back into your bed. You're CEO. Use your negotiation skills."

I frowned. "You want me to negotiate sex? Takes the fun out of it doesn't it?"

"You're good at mergers, so I'd think you'd be good at *this* kind of merger."

"Jesus, Dex. Are you drunk?"

"No. Merge in bed. Best merger you'll get these days."

"No bed. We did it in the back of the bar," I clarified.

"You... um... wow." I hadn't heard him sputter in a while.

"Right. Fine, it wasn't a one-night stand. It was a quickie."

"Yeah, gotcha. What's her name? Maybe we all know her."

"I'm not telling you her name. It doesn't matter, anyway. I'm in fucking Denmark and then I'll be in Asia. It's not like her pussy's anywhere near here for round two."

"But it could be."

I flopped my head back against the chair. "It was a *quickie*. I know barely anything about her."

"But do you want to know more?"

Yes. Yes, I did. I absolutely, one hundred percent, wanted more. Not just sex. I wanted to know about her family that drove her to drink wine alone. Wanted to fuck her while we were face-to-face so I could watch her when she came. I wanted to do–

A fuck ton.

The connection. The chemistry. Off. The. Charts.

Was I like Dex getting one look at Lindy and buying her a ring? No. But I was all in for more. Except–

"Doesn't matter, Dex. I'm based in Denver, not in

Hunter Valley, and I'm all over the world from one day to the next."

"This Hyport sale doesn't have to happen. I think James Corp's five hundred hotels, you'd think–"

"Five hundred and sixty-three."

He scoffed. "Right, more to my point. You'd think we had enough money."

"It's not about the money," I countered immediately. I was insistent on this deal and for reasons completely opposite of why any other CEO would want to take over another billion-dollar company. To give my father the fucking middle finger.

Now he sighed. "I know you're trying to clean up Dad's mess, but does it really matter?"

"Yes," I said immediately. "It's important to me that this deal with Hyport goes through. I want to right the wrong that Dad made. It's all about integrity. Honor."

"Not fucking the assistant," he added.

"Exactly. I'm cleaning up the image. Everything Rated G. No sex parties. Nothing inappropriate. No talk of two-person showers in the suites," I added so he'd know how tame and buttoned-up this all had to be.

"Shit, dude. Don't go there."

"Robert Hyport knows Dad as the fuck up that fucked everything. He knows me as the CEO who gets shit done. Who makes money. No kinky shit. No mixing sex and business."

"Okay, so don't mix them. You can still have the woman from Hunter Valley."

"Not when my dick and her pussy aren't in the same time zone." Unfortunately.

He laughed, but I didn't think he found me funny. "You don't think I know about long distance relationships? The only thing that doesn't work from far away is making a baby. Otherwise, it's all possible. I have two words for you: Video call sex."

"Great," I muttered. "Now I have an image of you jacking off to a computer camera."

"That's not all we do," he said, his usual mischief lacing his words.

I rubbed my eyes and wished sleep would come soon. "Fucker."

"All I'm saying is if you want her, you'll make it happen."

"I met a woman in a bar. In. A. Bar."

"Was she a hooker?"

I pulled my cell from my ear, stared at it for a second. "What? No."

"Then there's a chance."

"You're saying I can't have a relationship with a hooker?"

"Do you *want* a relationship with a hooker?"

I had to laugh. "Where the hell is this conversation going?"

"You said it wasn't going to work."

"How many one-night stands have you had? Wait... how many *quickies* have you had?"

He grunted. Yeah, that was what I thought. His rookie days in pro hockey had to have been filled with puck bunnies and quick fucks.

"How many of them did you think of after you zipped up and walked away?"

He still didn't say anything, so I pushed on.

"Then why are you all up in my business?"

"Because you're you, not a pro athlete with women offering their panties and BJs."

"Well, no puck bunnies around here. I'm CEO of James Corp. A relationship isn't happening. I have a to-do list a mile long. Hotels to run. I sign the paychecks for tens of thousands of people so they can buy groceries. I have a shit ton of responsibility."

My job was my life. My life was in Denmark. Singapore. Wherever. Definitely not in Eve's perfect, tight, wet, amazing pussy.

"You took a break from that responsibility, from the Hyport deal, long enough to fuck in a bar once, you can do it again."

"I don't want to have a string of quickies. I'm too old for that shit."

I had no idea why I was arguing with him about this. Maybe it was because I really wanted Eve, wanted more of her and not just face down over a desk, but was cranky because I couldn't have her and he was rubbing my face in it.

"Whatever, dude. You, your right hand and your dick, have fun tonight. Whisper sexy words in Danish to yourself as you jack off."

I hung up to him laughing. The asshole.

8

EVE

THE PAST THREE MORNINGS, I woke up at five and leapt
from the bed. Peeked out the window. No Mr. Big Dick.
The house behind mine was dark. I hadn't seen Silas–or
his dick–since the bar. I'd thought about it... him, non-
stop, since. When I'd ordered my glass of wine that night
and glanced at the guy sitting at the bar, I'd done a
double take. It had been him. My sexy wake-up alarm.
Clothed. And up close. I'd been stunned and had given
him a thorough once over. That beard. Those pale eyes.
Square jaw. Slightly tousled hair. Then his body–
clothed–was solid, well-muscled but still lean. His
clothes were high end, but not stuffy. Conservative but
stylish in an understated way. Pretty much, he looked

good without showing off or appearing like he was trying.

It took me a bit to catalog all the things about him that were panty melting.

He'd noticed and I'd flushed. But then he'd given me one in return and well... game on.

I never expected to have a few shots of tequila with the guy and have him fuck me over a desk, but... IT HAD BEEN AMAZING!

That dick I'd eyed before dawn? The quick glimpse I saw of it up close had been perfect. Big. *Really* big. Long. Thick. Veiny. Large crowned head. He could have been a dick model. Maybe he was. I had no idea. All I knew was that he knew how to wield that thing because I'd been *good* sore for a day. He hadn't gone gentle on me, not that I'd wanted that. I'd told him not to be. I'd never, *ever* had sex like that before. It had been mind-blowing. Unforgettable.

"Earth to Eve."

I blinked and smiled at Bridget Beckett.

"You okay?" she asked, cocking her head with a look of concern. That made her glasses slip and she pushed them up.

I grabbed the ten-dollar bill she held out and made change for her coffees. "Sorry, yeah, I'm fine. Just... thinking."

She wore a green puffy coat and had a knit hat on her

head. The forecast was for more snow, but that was pretty much the report from now until April. "The way you're blushing, it has to do with a guy. Maybe?"

My answer was my blush getting hotter. "Maybe."

Her whole face lit up. "Ooh, tell me!"

I shook my head, which made my earrings swing. Remembered how dark Silas's house was this morning. How I'd walked out of the bar back office with a *thanks* and not much more. I wasn't going to be a clinger or have false expectations that a little fun meant anything. Except I couldn't stop thinking about him.

"It was a one-time thing. It's over."

She drooped, as if I'd let the air out of her. "Oh, well, that's no fun."

"What's going on with you?"

"Besides working at the high school, Mav and I are tackling the philanthropic branch of James Corp. We're rolling out a local program now."

"Oh?" I turned and got to work on her coffee order.

She told me about it while my back was to her. "Small business loans here in Hunter Valley. We want to see more places like yours succeed. The part we both love about this town is that there aren't any big box stores or chains. Not downtown or out by the highway. The more local places succeed, the less chance those conglomerates will take over."

I glanced at her over my shoulder. "That's a great idea."

She nodded and I started to steam some milk, then poured it over the shots of espresso.

"Want a cup holder?" I asked, grabbing a few napkins.

With a head shake, she replied, "Nah, Mav's just outside with Scout."

I glanced out the picture window and saw Mav's broad back. In pink. "Is he in the coffee shop t-shirt?"

She rolled her eyes and nodded. "He loves that thing. And you two look like twins."

I glanced down at my outfit. Pink Steaming Hotties shirt–that matched Mav's–with a slouchy sweater over it and a pair of my favorite jeans. And yes, there was a small hole on the left knee.

"Isn't he cold?"

Grabbing the coffees, she said, "Mav? Nah, it's all that big dick energy that keeps him running hot."

She gave me a sly smile and a finger wave.

Big dick energy. I knew a guy who had that. My pussy clenched remembering.

9

SILAS

"I'M WORRIED ABOUT YOUR DICK," Theo told me.

"As a medical professional or as my brother?"

"Both."

"Why? What could possibly be wrong with it medically?"

"Gotta clean those pipes. And you can get carpal tunnel if you use your hand too much."

I had to laugh. "Jesus, Theo. You graduated med school?""

"What? Your pipes need cleaning."

I was cleaning my pipes solo just fine.

"You have no idea how much I want to *clean those pipes* but I'm on a different continent."

"Where the hell are you?"

"Singapore."

"I'm surprised your assistant doesn't have it penciled in on your calendar." I could picture him shaking his head in disappointment.

"If you've forgotten, Verna has you by the balls," I reminded. The older woman was the office manager for his medical clinic and was as ruthlessly proficient as Bradley.

He grunted because he knew I was fucking right.

"But I work eight to five these days. I'm home for sex o'clock with Mal every day."

"Sex o'clock?"

His laughter rang through the phone. It was new for him, and I liked hearing him so happy. "You know it, Si. I'm watching out for you."

"Me? No. You're watching out for my dick. You have way too much interest in it. *That's* not healthy."

He laughed again.

"And everyone called me the grumpy one," he said, then hung up.

"I can take care of getting laid on my own," I said aloud to myself when I tossed my cell aside.

If I had any interest in a woman–besides Eve–I'd pull up a woman's name from my contacts and take her out. Or to my bed. But the only pussy I wanted to sample a second time was Eve's. Fuck. I was getting hard thinking of her and how she'd clenched my dick so hard when she came that I saw Jesus, which meant I had a fucking problem where she was concerned.

Almost two weeks later and I was still thinking of her. Still remembering her taste.

I either needed to get back to Hunter Valley, find her and fuck her out of my system, or I needed to forget about her, which wasn't going to happen. Either. I wasn't going to forget what Eve and I shared, and I didn't think I'd ever get enough of her.

10

EVE

WITH MY HEAD inside the lower cabinet, I looked for the reason the wash sink was leaking. It wasn't much, just a trickle, but the batch of napkins that had been stored beneath were ruined. Fortunately, their destruction was what alerted us to the problem.

It was after three, which meant the quietest part of the day. Before I disappeared beneath the counter, there was only one customer working on his laptop by the window.

"Um, Eve," June, my afternoon employee and friend, said. I saw her sneakered feet out of the corner of my eye.

"What's up?" I asked, my voice strained since I was

bent funny. I had a wrench around the... whatever it was called that a wrench tightened.

"There's someone here to see you."

For a second, a thrill shot through me that it might be Silas. I'd been thinking about him and what we did on that desk pretty much non-stop. The fact that I was exhilarated at the possibility that he was here proved how much I liked him. Wanted him. Craved him.

I quickly squashed the idea that he was here. He didn't know who I was other than the woman from the bar. He didn't know I owned Steaming Hotties. Or lived behind him and watched him walk around naked. If we ran into each other on the street or at the grocery store, that'd be one thing, but he couldn't intentionally seek me out.

I maneuvered out of the cabinet, set the wrench down, and pulled myself to my feet using the edge of the counter for leverage. There, standing all smug and asshole-ish, was Cheney.

Inwardly, I groaned. He was the *last* person I wanted to see. "This is a surprise." It was a complete surprise, but he missed my sarcastic tone. "What brings you in?"

The only reason he was in town was because of me. His family lived up by the resort in a big, fancy house paid for by the family's mine. Yes, an actual mine. It was sold to a conglomerate, but the way they lived, they had to have made a lump sum and then now lived lavishly off of annual dividends.

I learned a long time ago that money meant nothing. Not happiness. Not friends. Sure, it helped pay the bills. I wouldn't begrudge anyone the desire for money. But when it was the only desire, when it turned someone… sour, then it was bad.

Money spoiled my parents. Cheney, too.

I wouldn't let it spoil me. I liked to think I was like my grandparents, earning my keep and building something from hard work.

June stood a few feet away with a stack of coffee filters. She looked like she was counting them, which was not something anyone ever did, so she was completely and totally eavesdropping. That was fine. I wanted this conversation witnessed because whatever was said was heading back to my parents and spun around to make me look like shit.

"I talked to your parents."

Gah.

He crossed his arms over his chest, making himself seem wider. That was impossible since he was built like a runner, but he didn't run. He had a trainer who he paid a fortune to teach him how to play squash. Squash!

He wore khakis, a heavy coat and boots that were meant for mountaineering. He was dressed like those living in tropical climates who drove a fancy 4x4 SUV

and never went off-roading or saw ice or snow. The coat
and boots would never be put to real use to do something as simple as shovel his own walkway. He wouldn't
want his slick dark hair and perfect mustache to get
messed up. I couldn't see his fingers, but I assumed his
nails were manicured. They always were.

Looking at him made me depressed. Not only
because he was annoying, but because I'd stayed with
him for years. Sure, I'd been at boarding school and
college at the time, so it had been a long-distance relationship, but we'd been *together*.

It took me too long to recognize he was shallow, arro-
gant, selfish, and didn't have any of my interests or feel-
ings at heart. To him, I was a trophy. A woman he wanted
on his arm. No, more than that. He wanted the alliance
with my parents. To be part of the Hunter family. The
family money he wanted to live on, even on top of his
own. The lifestyle I didn't give a shit about.

He didn't care about anyone but himself. Well, he
cared about my parents and that was creepy as hell.

"That's nice."

"Your mother said that you had no intention of giving
up on this little project of yours and moving home." He
looked around as he spoke.

As if the original brick walls and stylish interior was
me living chained to a tree I was trying to protect from
deforestation while on a hunger strike.

"This is my business, Cheney. My job. I'm an adult. Why would I move home?"

He leaned in, his dark gaze serious. Not intense.

Silas had been intense. His entire demeanor. The way he fucked. With deliberation and focus and he'd been thinking of my needs. What guy pulled out and ate a woman out to get her to come?

Silas.

The comparison between the two men was obvious. Cheney *tried* to be everything Silas actually was. That made me see my ex as more of a wuss than ever before.

"You're my woman, Evelyn."

Evelyn.

I frowned, stepped back. I was soooooo not his woman.

While the counter was between us, I wanted a little more room. He was like a spoiled kid with a toy he couldn't have. He'd do anything to get it, no matter the cost. I had a feeling the cost would be to me. Not him.

It was my turn to cross my arms.

"No, I'm definitely not your woman. I made that very clear last year when I told you we were breaking up, that we are no longer together. Please stop coming by because you are no longer in my life."

He raised a hand and pointed all around. "This place? Your little fun? It's done. Your father made me the executor on your trust fund."

June shoved the coffee filters away a little more aggressively than necessary and went to the urn of fresh coffee.

My stomach dropped. My grandparents left me money. Lots of it. I wasn't able to access the trust because of two conditions. The first was a little crazy: marriage. If I married, I could take control of my own trust. I always wondered why they'd set that stipulation and assumed it was because they founded the resort together and had an amazing marriage and wanted the same for me. Maybe if I found the perfect guy, we could use the money together to build something as enduring as my grandparents. There was no marriageable man on the horizon.

Definitely not the one in front of me.

Not even for access to my money. That meant I would only get control of it to use it for Steaming Hotties through the second condition: turning thirty.

I couldn't touch it until that age unless the executor granted special permission. My father had been the executor and he'd agreed for me to take money out to open Steaming Hotties. I'd thought it was because he liked my business idea, that my business plan I'd shared with him had been solid, but no. He'd done it to amuse me. He'd given me enough to get the business up and running, but not much more. I was expecting a second payment next month, but after the call the other day, I

got worried. Pulling together all the paperwork necessary, I applied for a small business loan at the banks.
Local ones and a national chain in Missoula.

I was glad I started that process because I wondered
if my father ever planned to give me the second infusion
of cash. It was becoming really clear he'd had this
worked out with Cheney all along to force me to quit.

To let me have my fun and then shut it down.

"Why?" I asked. The question was all-encompassing,
but Cheney knew what I meant.

"Because he wants us together," he replied, as if it
was actually that simple.

"By controlling my finances?" That made no sense.
Seriously. None. Why would a woman ditch a business
she'd worked hard to establish and make flourish, solely
because a man she dumped took over control of her trust
fund?

It was my money. Mine.

I didn't want to lounge by the pool at the club and
play doubles tennis. I wanted to work. To be like my
grandparents and build something of my own. That was
why I'd used that money instead of a small business loan
from a bank. *It was my money.*

He shrugged, but not because he didn't know, but
because it was a done deal. As if my questions were irrel-
evant. "You'll get an allowance when we marry, so what's
the difference? It's to ensure you don't make poor deci-

sions. Consider this practice. Oh, and Evelyn, this place is a poor decision."

I swallowed hard and tried not to reach across the counter and strangle him. Poor decision, my ass. I was *looking* at the biggest poor decision of my life. Him.

"It's turning a profit," I said. It was, but barely. I couldn't live off it... yet.

"Not for long. Not without that next infusion of cash, right?" He looked around. "You've got payroll. Coffee beans can't be cheap. Including that stupid pink t-shirt you're wearing." He eyed my chest where the Steaming Hotties logo stretched across my boobs. "I'm sure the landlord won't hold out until your thirtieth birthday for rent because as executor, I'm not giving you another dime toward this... bad choice."

He was trying to force me to shut down.

"I don't need my trust fund to run the business," I told him, tipping my chin up, hoping I showed the confidence I didn't feel. I didn't need it specifically. I needed money.

"Really?" he asked, his brow turning up, which made his mustache twitch. Had it always looked so stupid? "I guess I'll have to wait and see."

"You came in to tell me this? You could have done it over the phone. Saved yourself some time." I tipped my head down and looked at his clothes. "And the cost of a new outfit."

June came to stand beside me and slid a cup of coffee across the counter toward Cheney. It was in a to-go cup, lid already on. "Here you go," she said, her friendly customer-facing smile in place.

Cheney looked at the drink as if it was poison. "What's this?"

"Coffee. *To go.* You're leaving, aren't you?"

It was her turn to cross her arms and give him a look of death.

Cheney took the drink, took a big sip and gave me a sly smile. "See you soon, honey."

I watched through the picture window as he left the store, strolled down the sidewalk, taking another sip as he went.

"I hate that guy," June said. She'd never met him before, only heard about him from the times we drank wine and ate pizza together.

I turned my head. She was my first hire. My first friend in town after college. She was a year older and was a ski instructor who worked for me full time while waiting for the ski season to start.

"I hate him, too," I said, seething.

"What are you going to do?"

I frowned, grabbed the short sticks of pasta that we offered as compostable coffee stirrers and started shoving them in their little container. "I'm not marrying him, that's for fucking sure."

"Good." She turned away. "Don't listen to him. The t-shirts are great. Makes your boobs look spectacular."

I humphed because I was too angry to outright agree.

Next, I grabbed a rag and started wiping down the counter, but it didn't need it. I needed something to do with my hands.

"Oh, Eve."

I turned. "Yeah?"

"I put some of this in his coffee." She held up a bottle of powdered laxative and waggled her eyebrows.

My mouth dropped open, and I snagged it from her. It was half empty. "Where did you get that?"

"My aunt is having a colonoscopy in a few days and needs this as part of the prep, which sounds pretty awful. I picked it up for her at the store on the way in." She eyed the plastic bottle and frowned, probably at the idea of getting a camera up her butt. "I'll have to get a replacement bottle, but it's so worth it."

"Why on earth do you have it here behind the counter?" I wondered.

She tipped her chin down, gave me a stare. "Just say thank you."

I envisioned Cheney on the toilet for the foreseeable future and I had to smile.

"Thank you." I gave her a hug, the laxative bottle between us. "You're such a good friend."

11

EVE

A FEW DAYS LATER, June came in at eleven, as usual, and slapped the newspaper down on the counter.

"I solved your problem," she said, coming around the counter to join me.

"Oh? I'm not stripping." Since Cheney had come in, we'd brainstormed all my earning options. She'd tossed out stripping as a possibility since I had really nice boobs. She'd been joking, although my boobs were a good feature.

She eyed me, then pointed at the paper.

I grabbed it up, scanned it. "The parade of lights?" The front page talked about the annual winter parade that happened the first Saturday in December. "We're always open for that."

"Flip it over," she said, washing her hands at the sink. I did. "Oh."

"James Corp is offering low-interest small business loans to locals," she explained. "It's an amazing opportunity for the community. You should apply. I'm sure you'll get accepted and get that capital infusion you need."

For the first time in days, I felt... hope. I checked with my lawyer and my father had made the dickhead the executor of my trust fund. I couldn't touch a dime of it without Cheney's approval–which I wasn't going to get–before I turned thirty. The only other option was to marry and it sure as hell wasn't going to be him.

I was not going to be a trophy wife. I wasn't going to wile away my life. I wanted to work. To go to bed at night exhausted because of what I'd accomplished, not because I'd shopped too much. If I was going to marry someone just for the hell of it, it'd be Mr. Big Dick because I might as well get something out of the arrangement.

Steaming Hotties income was good, but not good enough to float rent. Or the bills for coffee beans. Paper towels. I couldn't pay June or any of the other part-timers for much longer.

"Bridget told me about this, and I completely forgot." I spun and faced her. "I've already got a contract with

Mav to supply the coffee for the inn when it opens. He's seen my business plan."

She pointed at the paper in my hand. "You definitely have to do it. Then you won't have to strip."

I took a deep breath, smiled. "I'd rather strip than shut down out of principle alone. I will not see an ex lord money over me. No way. And my parents can suck it."

"You go, girl. Reach out to Bridget."

I grabbed my phone and texted her.

12

SILAS

"CHANGE OF SCHEDULE FOR TODAY. You're headed to Hunter Valley."

Bradley was in my ear and I was in my apartment in Denver brewing a cup of coffee. I finished my call with London and was waiting to be added to a phone meeting with the Hyport team in Geneva.

"I thought I was meeting with the linen association downtown," I said, holding the mug and waiting impatiently for the percolating to finish.

"You're doing interviews for the James Corp loan program with Bridget," he replied. "They start at ten."

It wasn't six and I was supposed to be in Montana in four hours.

I sighed, rubbed a hand down my face. "This is Mav's project. Why am I tackling it?"

I wasn't bothered about missing a lunch with the linen association president, but why did I have to take on Mav's work, too? It was pretty much a whine like a five-year-old. I had the usual CEO business like linen lunches, but I had so much to do on the Hyport deal, I didn't want to do Mav's work, too.

"He's in the San Juans. Some issue with the inn there."

He was in Washington state, not Montana. Great.

"No delay possible, instead?" I wondered. The machine beeped and I filled my mug.

"No delay. Bridget's ready to go with these last ones. She's not a James... yet and wants one of you to be there."

"Theo is in town," I reminded.

"Theo's got patients."

"I have a meeting with the linen association and whatever else you haven't yet told me about."

"I cleared your schedule. You're in Hunter Valley today."

"What about Dex?"

"Tampa."

I sighed again, then took a careful sip. It was good coffee, but nothing like the beans that were stocked at my small place in Hunter Valley.

"I had the pilot put in a flight plan to return at four. You'll be home by dinner."

The caffeine was slowly kicking in. Hmm... wait. Why was I so grumpy about Mav being away and Theo having too many patients to do the interviews when I could see Eve? This was the perfect opportunity to see her again.

I didn't want to be back in this boring apartment by dinner. I could be with Eve just like Dex and Theo kept prodding me about.

For the first time in two weeks, since I flew out of Hunter Valley last, I was excited. So was my dick.

"I'll stay overnight," I told him. I wanted her in my bed and for a hell of a lot more than a quickie. I wanted naked, sweaty, loud sex with Eve.

My place in Hunter Valley was ready for me, although I didn't remember if I made the bed before I left the last time. The heat could be adjusted remotely. Same went with the security, the lights, including the lock to the front door. I just needed Eve.

"All right," he replied, always willing to shift and flex. "Then you'll fly from there directly to San Francisco to be on schedule for tomorrow's noon meeting with the US Hyport team."

I understood Bridget's need for me today. She was involved in doling out money that wasn't hers. There was no question Mav would put some kind of prenup in place when they got married, which was definitely going to happen, but this was corporate cash, not Mav's personal income. Besides, she was giving it to small businesses for local growth, not to renovate a kitchen or a girl's trip to the Maldives.

If my brothers weren't available, I needed to be. But I could also have some fun... and orgasms.

"Fine."

"Put that coffee in a to-go cup and put some pants on. The plane leaves in forty-five."

13

EVE

EVER SINCE I submitted the online form for the James Corp Hunter Valley Small Business Advancement Program, I'd been antsy and eager for the interview.

Bridge reached out and said after reviewing my application it was a done deal, especially the way Mav loved my coffee, but the papers weren't signed. The money wasn't in my bank account. Which meant Cheney and his threats still loomed over me.

I hadn't heard from him since he left the shop that day. I wasn't sure if it was because he was still in the bathroom or if he was expecting me to crawl back to him and my parents.

Either way, I didn't care. I just wanted him out of my

life for good. While he was executor, I didn't have to deal with him if I didn't want money from the trust. I'd get it in a few years. I could leave it untouched until then.

I walked into the building that held the James Corp Hunter Valley office jittery and nervous as if I'd had a Devil's Brew triple espresso. I detoured to the ladies' restroom beside the elevator and stood in front of the mirror.

"You can do this. You can do this. It's this or Cheney," I whispered, looking myself in the eye. I dressed fairly conservatively, considered what a banker might wear and dressed accordingly. I wasn't wearing a Steaming Hotties pink tee to a loan meeting. "Fuck Cheney."

With that, I spun around and made my way across the hall.

A woman at the reception desk greeted me warmly.

"You must be Evelyn," she said.

I smiled back. "Eve."

"I love your coffee," she said. "I'm Jemma. They're waiting for you. Just head in there." She swiveled in her chair and pointed to an open conference room door.

"Thanks, Jemma."

When I crossed the office, I overheard Bridge through the open door. "No, mashed potatoes can't have lumps. It's against the law."

"Against the law?"

I stepped into the doorway, listening to the weird

conversation my friend was having with someone. A man.

When I leaned in, afraid to interrupt, even though the topic definitely wasn't about work, I saw it wasn't just any man.

It was Silas.

Mr. Big Dick.

"Eve! Hey!" Bridget stood from the huge conference table and came around to me.

I ignored her and kept staring at Silas. In his suit. And tie.

He stared at me right back.

"It's you," he murmured, with complete surprise on his face. His gorgeous, bearded face. The smile that slowly spread meant he was happy to see me.

"Oh shit. What are you doing here?" I asked, then winced. Not the best first line for an interview, but THIS WAS SILAS. MR. BIG DICK. Dressed, thank God.

I tried to process why he'd be in this meeting, and it wasn't computing. Not fast enough, at least.

Bridget gave me a hug, albeit an awkward one since I didn't really hug her back. I could only ogle Silas because he was more handsome than I remembered.

"You two know each other?" Bridget asked, stepping back and looking between us. She pushed her glasses up her nose as if seeing better would make her understand what was between us. Which, a few weeks ago, had only been a condom.

"Yeah," Silas said, scratching the back of his neck. Was that a blush that crept up his cheeks? It was hard to tell with his close-cut beard. Why? I'd been the one bent over a desk being fucked. "We met the last time I was in town."

"Oh. Well, that's handy. Silas is helping me with the interviews today since Mav is out of town."

Why was he helping? "Silas..."

"James," he finished.

"Silas *James?*" I asked, stunned. He was Mav's and Theo's brother? Holy shit.

He looked nothing like either of them. Mav was dark. Silas was fair. He was also a few inches shorter and less stocky, which wasn't that hard to do since Mav was built like a Viking.

"Evelyn Hunter," Silas clarified, his gaze raking over me. "You own Steaming Hotties."

"You read the applications on the plane, didn't you?" Bridget asked him, worried he hadn't prepared.

"Yes, but it wasn't completed by *Eve.* I definitely would have remembered."

"Only a few people call me by my legal name," I explained. "I prefer Eve."

"This is just a formality, really, since Mav approved

your application for the business loan," Bridget said, going around the table. "Sit, please."

Silas pulled out a chair for me. Silas, the guy I'd had sex with. The guy I watched walking around his house naked. The guy I hadn't known was Mav's brother. Or a James. Or one of the men who'd be responsible for my business loan.

Shit. *Shit.* Shit!

"Wait," I said, holding up my hand. They froze. "I... I can't take the money."

Bridget dropped into her seat as if she weighed a ton. "What? Why not? Do you no longer need it?"

I looked to Silas. "I can't take money from a guy I've— that we've..."

Shit. I had to explain myself, my reasoning for turning down a legitimate, small business-favorable loan. Except I didn't want to tell Bridge that I'd had sex with her possible future brother-in-law. That I had been thinking about more with him and that seeing him in person again only made the need to be with him that much more urgent. But I didn't kiss and tell, and I didn't want to have to do it now.

Silas shut the conference room door, then leaned against it. It reminded me of him pressing me into the one at the bar.

"That you've..." Bridget said, letting it hang.

Silas gave me a piercing glance and somehow

decided since I brought it up, he'd be okay to share. "Bridge, Eve and I met the last time I was in town."

"That's what you said. I don't see why that's a problem bec– Oh."

She looked at us differently now, not with confusion, but with... mirth? Amusement.

"Yes, oh," I replied, trying to stay professional when a part of me wanted to go over and sniff Silas's neck, then run my hands over him. Maybe grip his dick and feel how big he was.

Focus. Focus!

"And um... because we... *oh'd*, I can't take the money."

"Why the hell not? You need the money. You should take it. Problem solved," Silas said, pushing off the door and standing before me. Close. Too close. I breathed in his clean scent. Soap or aftershave or something yummy. "What we did has nothing to do with this." He waved his hand around the conference room.

"It has everything to do with it," I countered, tapping my foot on the carpeted floor.

"How?"

I stepped right in front of him, tipped my chin back so I could look him in the eye and whispered, "We had sex. I won't have a former lover lording money over me."

"Former?" he whispered back. "Who said anything about *former*? I had to travel for work. I assure you my dick is more than ready to get back inside you. And now that I know who you are, besides just *Eve,* we can–"

"That's what you got from what I said?" I hissed. "Former?"

He grinned, those pale eyes roving over my face as if re-memorizing me. As if he found me fascinating. Intriguing. He was studying me the same way he had that night. Before we had a few shots of tequila. And after.

"Former is a very specific word. That indicates the past," he added. "If that's what you want, only the one time where I made you come again and again while I bent you over a–"

"I'm still in the room," Bridget interrupted. "While you're both whispering, I can hear you. And please never mention your dick in front of me again."

I closed my eyes and wanted a sinkhole to open up.

I spun away from Silas's gorgeousness and his delicious smell and all the things about him that made my panties wet and faced Bridget, still seated at the table.

"A... relationship, past or present, doesn't disqualify you for the loan. It's a legal and binding contract with James Corp, not Silas specifically. Please explain why you have to turn down the loan," she repeated. "Did Silas do something wrong? Did he–"

I held up my hand. "No. Silas was a perfect gentleman."

He huffed from behind me. "I wasn't a gentleman at all, and you liked it that way."

Bridget rolled her eyes. "Okay, I'm going to step out and let you two work this out." She gave a little finger wave and left, shutting the conference room door behind her.

That left me with Silas... and another desk.

I swallowed hard, trying to stay on task. Silas smelled good. Looked good. And I remembered how good he felt. Deep inside. My pussy clenched in anticipation of a repeat. It was one thing to have sex where a random bar patron–or owner since we'd been in his office–may have interrupted us, but it was another to do it now with Bridget outside the door.

"I applied for the loan because my other source of investment money has been cut off." I wasn't going to waste their time explaining how dysfunctional my family was.

"Fuck, Eve. We didn't get a chance to share contact info before you left the bar. You pretty much blew my mind. Please say you want to do it again," he said, his intense gaze raking down my body, just like it had that night in the bar. My nipples hardened and I was sure he could see them through my top. "Because while I've been away, I've thought about it."

I blinked. "You want more?" I didn't know why I was so surprised. Well, maybe I did. We'd had a lot to drink.

While I hadn't been drunk, the tequila had definitely lowered my inhibitions. I held no expectation that a quickie over a desk in the back of a bar was more than just that. Sex with an almost-stranger.

Except he clearly wanted more and now he definitely wasn't a stranger. He was Silas James. The CEO of James Corp, but also Bridget's boyfriend's brother. The way she and Mav were hot and heavy... and seriously together, he was probably her future brother-in-law.

So he wasn't a rando. He was definitely vetted by my friend.

He had a job. He had a stable income. I mentally laughed that *stable income* meant he was a billionaire. He had three brothers I knew and liked. He also had been gentle and commanding and very, very filthy when it came to sex. Actually, not that gentle at all. That had been us with only the most important parts of our bodies bare for fucking. No bed. Nothing. I could only imagine what he'd be like if we had time... and privacy.

He stared at me in return, as if it was impossible I wasn't considering a repeat. "Feel my dick and you tell me how much I want more. Don't you?"

I licked my lips since they were suddenly dry as I glanced down and saw how hard he was. It was impossible to miss that steel beam in his pants. My pussy was getting wet, getting ready to take that big thing again.

"Well, yeah, but that proves my point all the more. I can't have sex with you again–"

"Not just one more time. *Many* times." He leaned down, pretty much growled. "I don't think I'll get enough of you anytime soon. I mean, we were... explosive."

Explosive. Absolutely.

I whimpered, swallowed hard. "See, this."

"What?" He reached out, stroked my hair and I closed my eyes. Reveled in the slightest bit of contact. My nipples hardened. My body was a flipping traitor!

"I can't have lots of sex with you and take a loan. It'll feel like... like payment."

"This isn't a payment for personal interactions, it's a business loan. You have to pay it back, with interest, although the terms are very favorable."

I laughed the way he sounded like a banker or a CEO trying to close a deal and tossed my hands up.

"It's still not happening," I replied, resolved. Resigned. Aroused. "The loan. The sex, sure. Definitely. Tell Bridget sorry, but I'll find the money I need to stay afloat elsewhere."

"Wait. If I hadn't been here, if Mav had instead, then you'd have taken the loan," Silas said. He was in jeans, leather boots, and a pale blue dress shirt with the sleeves rolled up. Why was a man's forearm so hot? It was like catnip to my pussy. One look and it was ready to go crazy.

I nodded. "Yes, but once I found out you two were related, that you're also a James, and not just any James, but the *CEO of James Corp* who is giving out the loans, then I'd have paid it all back immediately."

"So if you'd have slept with Dex or Theo it wouldn't be an issue since they don't work for James Corp."

I shrugged, not sure what I would have done. Both men were hot. Heck, all four James brothers were rugged and gorgeous. But I wasn't hot for Dex or Theo. I wanted Silas.

"Doesn't matter. Hypothetical," I reminded.

"You can't be serious. Really? You won't take the loan?"

I set my hands on my hips. I thought my words had been very clear.

"We had sex, Silas. You want more sex. And you would give me money. I can't do both. I won't accept the loan. Sorry."

The clock was ticking. My bank account was shrinking, and rent was coming due. Bills were going to start to build and within a week or two I couldn't cover all of them. I might have more amazing sex with Mr. Big Dick, but what was I going to do about my bills?

I turned to leave, but he hooked my arm.

"Fine," he said, although he didn't look too happy agreeing. "No loan. Then sex."

My mouth opened, but I didn't know what to say. "I... I..."

"Was that one time in the bar enough for you?" He switched topics so fast I had whiplash.

I sputtered. "Um... well–"

"It wasn't for me. All the time I was away I thought about it. Us. *You.*" He pulled me close, and his hands began to roam. One went up my back, the other down to cup my butt. Oh my. "I still remember what you taste like. What you feel like around me when you come. How perfect this ass is."

"Oh," I said, staring at the soft whiskers on his chin.

"Eve," he murmured, forcing my gaze up to meet his. "Ready for more?"

His nearness and his scent were messing with me. With my hands on his chest, I felt his heart beating. When he pulled me closer still, I felt him hard and thick against my hip. My pussy clenched in eagerness. Except... "The loan–"

He lowered his head, ran his nose along my neck, licked the curve of my ear.

"No loan. Just... more. Do you want more, Eve?"

The way he said the word *more* made me melt. My panties, too. That one word could mean so much.

"Yes," I whispered, because I wanted all the possibilities of more.

One of Silas's hands left me and yanked open the door. "Bridge, take Jemma out for lunch."

"What?" she replied. "Why? Oh...here? Are you going to–"

"Yes." He slammed the door on the rest of Bridget's words.

Then kissed me.

14

SILAS

SHE WOULDN'T TAKE the loan. Fine. I respected her for that choice. It was smart, considering. But I wasn't giving up the chance of more sex. More of her body. More of how she responded to my touch. To my dick fucking her hard. With the way she was kissing me back, she wanted it just as much. I spun us around so she was sitting on the edge of the conference room table, shoving chairs out of the way with my thighs.

"Silas, another table?" she asked when I lifted my head.

Her lips were glossy and swollen, her breaths coming in little pants. Cupping her ass, I pulled her close so her legs straddled my hips. I could feel the heat of her core through our clothes.

"Another table."

She wasn't wearing a dress this time, but black dress pants with a plum-colored turtleneck. Professional, conservative, and appropriate for the winter weather outside. But not user friendly for fucking.

"Here?"

I met her gray gaze. "Here."

No way was I waiting.

"Two weeks was too long. Fuck, I can't resist you. I don't want to."

She reached for the buttons on my shirt. "You need to invest in snap shirts," she said, remembering our conversation from the bar.

I couldn't agree more because the stupid buttons were delaying her hands on me.

Yanking the hem of her turtleneck, it came free of her pants and I pushed it up beneath her arms, exposing her tits.

"Fuck, do your panties match?" The bra was a deep plum, almost identical to her top. But it was lacy, and I could see her nipple through the dainty material.

"Please say you're going to find out," she replied, arching her back.

Yes, yes I was. I always saw things through to completion and she'd be very well satisfied.

Using my fingers, I tugged the cup down, her nipple popping free.

Her hands stopped when I latched onto that hard tip. Sucked, then nipped at it.

So the other one didn't get neglected, I tugged on it, then pinched.

"Silas!" she moaned, thrusting her chest up.

"Shh," I whispered, although I had no doubt Bridget cleared the office.

I'd never done anything like this in a James Corp building before, but Eve drove me to forget I was CEO. I stilled, my hands hovering over her soft skin.

I groaned because I should be the example. The one whose propriety was above board. Behaving like this was what my father would do. Close the deal with his dick.

Except I hadn't known she was a loan applicant when we'd had sex. I hadn't been at work and there was no deal to close since she took it off the table.

And I was going to fuck her on one.

Unlike my father and his myriad of conquests, I saw Eve as more than just a quick lay. Even though we couldn't seem to keep our hands off each other, she was so much more than that.

"Silas?" she asked, breaking into my thoughts.

My hands cupped her breasts, and I was thinking about my father. I was not him. I got my head back in the game because she was fucking perfect, and I wouldn't let the asshole who molded me into the CEO I was today to be in this room with us.

I gave her a smile and gave Eve and her gorgeous tits all my attention. That got her writhing and moaning.

"Shh. You don't want anyone to hear," I added, switching to her other nipple.

My dick was throbbing and my balls ached to empty into Eve. The inner caveman was telling me to fuck. Rut. Claim. I'd never felt like this before. This out of control. This crazy.

"No one's here," she replied, letting her head fall back. The motion jutted out her chest and she filled my palms to overflowing.

"You sure about that?" I asked, glancing up at her. "The mailman could come in at any time and hear your breathy cries and pants. Know you're about to get fucked good and hard. That you need it."

I grinned as she flushed, then closed her eyes.

"Oh my God. You are a filthy talker."

"Yes, and you love it."

"Yes. But you need to hurry because I need that big dick."

I wasn't the only filthy talker. While I knew she *wanted* sex, having her say she *needed* my dick was a whole new level of insanely hot.

"Those pants are like a chastity belt," I commented.

She undid the leather buckle on her belt–regular, not

chastity–then the button, zipper. She wriggled her pants, along with her matching plum panties, down her long legs.

I opened my pants, lowered my boxers enough for my dick to spring free.

"Are you a dick model?" she asked, shoving her pants down, but struggling since she had her shoes on.

I laughed as I grabbed a condom from my wallet and stared down at it. "Dick model?"

I hadn't compared size to others in a locker room since high school, but I knew I was big. Women hadn't complained before, but I also hadn't had such a rave, eager review before either.

I stroked it and she froze, watching a bead of pre-cum bead at the slit.

She reached out, swiped it with her finger and sucked it off.

"Yes. It's perfect. It fills me up so good."

"Holy shit," I murmured, watching. "You have ten seconds to get those pants off because I'm getting in that pussy."

As I slid the condom on, she scrambled and only got one leg free, the fabric inside out and dangling around the other ankle. Parting her thighs, she laid back on her elbows. Her tits were lifted out of her bra, her pussy glistening and swollen, eager for my dick.

Stepping close, I swiped the head up and down her

slit, parting her, tapping her eager clit with it. I shifted, getting inside her by about an inch.

"Fuck."

Banding my arms about her back, I lifted her off the table then pulled her down onto me, pretty much impaling her with my entire length.

"Yes!" she cried, hooking her ankles behind my back.

I lowered her, still with my forearms behind her back and fucked her.

"Harder," she moaned.

She wanted harder? I'd give her harder.

I stood upright, gripped her hips and gave her a fucking to remember. The sound of her moans and the slap of flesh filled the room. Her tits wobbled from the pounding. She felt so fucking good, my balls were tight and ready to spill in her.

I'd never had sex like this before. Wild. Desperate.

She was the prettiest thing I'd ever seen. The abandon and the way she gave herself over to me was unbelievable. This wasn't just a fun quickie. This wasn't getting off.

This was...

"This is fucking insane," I breathed.

"I know. I had no idea it could be like this."

With one hand holding her in place, I set the other low on her belly and worked her clit with my thumb. I remembered from the last time she needed clit stimulation to get off.

And she did.

"Yes. Yes. Yes. Yes," she chanted, then her inner muscles clamped down.

And she screamed.

Someone was going to call the fire department. The police. Hell, dogs could hear that sound in a neighboring county.

I grinned as I shut my eyes, thrust as deep as I could go, and came. I pumped and pumped my cum into that condom, hoping it would hold.

"Holy fuck."

I set my hand on the table beside her head and kissed her.

Because I couldn't resist.

I was in big trouble here. I was addicted.

"Better than coffee," she murmured, sprawled on the table, messy and sweaty and her clothes a tangle around her. She truly looked well fucked.

Yeah, I did that.

"Huh?"

"Good dick is so much better than coffee."

I didn't know what that meant, but I figured coming from a coffee shop owner it was a compliment.

15

SILAS

"I can't believe you slept with my coffee supplier," Mav grumbled, dropping his overnight bag on the floor just inside the kitchen of his house. "And in the conference room."

Scout circled and jumped around him with excitement, his master finally home.

"Dex and Theo were all worried about my dick while I was gone and now you're upset that I got laid."

Bridget weaved around Scout's wriggling body and Mav lifted her up for a kiss that went on and on.

"Enough you two," I said, taking a pull from my beer.

I was at the kitchen island finishing up a meal of leftovers Bridget had pulled from the fridge.

Bridget called Mav, probably right after I kicked her out of the conference room and gave him the lowdown. I was sure it wasn't part of their philanthropy plan to have people turn the money down because of sex with one of the beneficiaries. Or to have sex with one *after* she turned the deal down. I had to wonder if they considered that. I certainly hadn't.

Of course, Dex, Theo, and Mav had their dicks on lockdown.

It was me. I was the problem. Although I didn't consider anything Eve and I did on that conference table–or the desk at the bar–a problem.

"You're one to talk," Mav said, coming up for air.

I grinned. "Did you come back from Washington so quickly because of my sex life? I'm touched."

"Fucker. As for me kissing my woman, this is our house," Mav grumbled, his big hand on Bridget's ass. They'd been apart less than two days and he was ready to toss me out on the front steps. To be honest, I understood how he felt because I wanted Eve, and I wanted her now. "Not the office." He gave me a pointed look.

"Do not tell me the two of you haven't gotten it on at the office," I countered.

The way Bridget tucked her face into Mav's neck was all the answer I needed.

"If you don't want to watch us make out, then go home." He was all growly and cranky sounding, but I had a feeling it had more to do with me currently cock-blocking him than me and my sex life.

After Eve and I pulled ourselves together and she'd walked out of the conference room with her hair mussed and walking a little funny, she headed back to Steaming Hotties. My afternoon schedule had kept me on a lock-down of calls and meetings so by the time I could meet up with her, Steaming Hotties was closed. I texted her at the number she gave me before she left.

> I want you in my bed. No more table sex. Next you'll be on top. I can watch your tits bounce as you ride me.

I hadn't heard back. Yet.

I didn't have a woman to return to after a business trip like Mav did. Not really a home either, as he snarled. I had the little miner's shack in town and my apartment in Denver. But I was rarely at either place. When I opened my eyes in the morning, I usually had no idea where I was. A different bed, different sheets, different showers, different everything almost every day.

"Then don't be cranky with me about sleeping with your coffee supplier," I countered. Then I paused. "Wait. How come you're not pissed because I slept with someone from the office?"

He set Bridget back on her feet, gave her a kiss on the top of her head before she turned to settle into her seat beside me. He got a swat to her ass in before she got far, and she giggled.

Fuck me.

He stared at me. "What the fuck are you talking about?"

"You're pissed I slept with your coffee supplier."

"Yes."

"Because I'm like Dad?"

He stilled. A guy his size should be like an aircraft carrier and take miles to come to a stop, but he literally froze.

"Like Dad?" he said, barely above a whisper. "Are you crazy?"

I ran a hand through my hair. "Well?"

"You're not like Dad. Jesus. Not one fucking thing about you is like him."

"I made you a plate. It's in the microwave," Bridget told him, her voice soft, perhaps trying to soothe him.

"Fine."

"You obviously think you're like Dad. Is this some kind of trauma bullshit?"

I had to laugh. "Definitely trauma bullshit."

When I grew up, I wanted to be a mechanic. Fix cars. I spent time with the chauffeur and helped him change the oil. Learned about replacing spark plugs. Simple stuff. My father found out and didn't go ballistic. Only laughed at me. Shamed me and my interest. Then fired the chauffeur.

After college, when I was working under him at James Corp, I turned a blind eye that he fucked everything with tits. Employee, client, waitress, flight attendant. It didn't matter. When he died, I vowed to run James Corp with solid leadership and no sexual harassment suits.

"What's the deal? I mean the loan, not the sex. She really won't take it?" Mav asked, opening the microwave to peek inside, lifting the lid on the splatter cover. Clearly he thought comparing myself to our father was over.

"Dude. Eve," he prompted when I didn't respond. "She wouldn't take it?"

Oh, she *took it,* but that wasn't what he meant.

He shut the door and pressed a few buttons to warm the food some more. Scout was still at his heels, so Mav squatted down to pet him while he waited.

"No. I guess her money source dried up," Bridget said.

Bridget didn't have billions in the bank like Mav and I. Her parents died when she was a kid and her sister, Lindy, had raised her. There had been some money since they kept the house after the accident, but not tons. No trust fund. Maybe a little life insurance. Bridget was frugal. In fact, she was finally coaxed into replacing her old beater car. It'd taken Mav a few months to gift her such a big present.

"You accepted her for the loan, so I'm not sure why a bank wouldn't. I'll have Bradley look into it," I said, wanting to know what the hell was up with that. If her original loan source wouldn't give her more, why turn down the James Corp loan? Who turned down a solid, low interest loan, especially when it was needed?

Eve.

"No, you will not," Bridget said, pointing at me with her fork. "Eve can turn this down if that's what she wants."

"Sex or not, I'm not going to mess with the loan," I said.

"I know that, but she clearly doesn't trust you," Bridget added. "Or merging her sex and business lives."

"I like her coffee shop," Mav grumbled. "Don't fuck with her."

I held up my hands. "As you said, I'm *fucking* her. Not fucking her over."

"Still..." she tossed out.

"I didn't force her, and I don't like you thinking I'm an asshole. She was right there with me. She made the decision to stay in that conference room with me."

Why was I explaining myself?

"The first time, at the bar, we didn't share more than first names. I didn't know her long enough to get last names or that she ran the coffee shop. Bridge, you saw her earlier. She had no idea who I was either when she came for the meeting."

"Not long enough? Dude, got staying problems?"

I frowned at Mav. "What? Fuck no. Ever heard of a quickie?"

"She won't take money from an ex, so she's a no-go," Bridget said, ignoring the brotherly barbs.

"I had sex with her seven hours ago. I'm *not* an ex," I repeated.

"I didn't want to get together with Mav because of sex," Bridge said.

"No, baby." Mav reached out, took her hand and kissed the knuckles. "You wanted sex, but you didn't want to fuck your boss."

"Oh, I wanted to fuck you, but I wasn't going to put myself in a situation where sex was going to be held over me as a power play. And Eve doesn't want that either."

I frowned, shoved a bite of pasta into my face. I wasn't an ex. An ex didn't keep having sex with her, so I would classify myself in the role of... friend with benefits? Quickie partner? No, that was too thin. Too simple for what we were. For what we did together. What we felt. It was complicated because I craved that woman. Loved her wild ways. Her passion and lack of inhibition. I wanted more. My dick was getting hard at the possibility alone.

I wanted her in a bed, with her on top.

If she texted back.

When was that going to happen? If she didn't respond soon, I'd miss her. Waiting until morning when the coffee shop opened to see her again wasn't an option because I flew out first thing for San Francisco. I had my life organized by Bradley down to the minute. And there were no minutes in Hunter Valley anytime soon. Not beyond tonight.

16

EVE

THERE HE WAS. Making coffee. Naked. Silas James. Still no curtains and his back door was all glass. Since my alarm went off and I started watching, he'd walked through the hallway several times. Four, actually, since I was counting. Full frontal–and rear–action. I didn't see him in fine detail like I had in the conference room, but I wasn't complaining.

I whimpered, wanting him again. I hadn't stopped thinking about him. Yesterday, in the James Corp office? Oh my God. I wasn't sure if I could look Bridget in the eye ever again.

It had been worth it. Sooooooo worth it.

Silas and I were good together. The chemistry was

insane. There was no denying it. He felt the same way. He'd pretty much said so.

I wanted him. I wanted more of that huge package that hung thick and heavy between his sturdy thighs. His intensity. Dirty talk. The way he couldn't seem to control himself with me.

I wondered if I made the right decision turning down the James Corp loan. It would be a binding contract. There would be terms. Interest. Silas wouldn't be lording anything over me like I said because if I met the rules of the deal, there was nothing he could do.

No. NO!

He was a billionaire. They had lawyers. Their lawyers had lawyers. If they wanted to fuck with me, they could. They could find something about the contract, some tiny loophole and I might lose my business.

I didn't think Silas was that kind of guy. Bridget liked him so I had to have faith in her nice-meter to trust that things were on the up-and-up. But last night, Cheney had called, and he made me question all men. It went like this:

"How's the business going?"

"Fine."

"Really? I'd think your bills are coming due."

"Yes. And then they're paid. That's how credit works."

"Mmm, well, when we're married, you won't have to work

or worry about bills. Or making coffee for others. You won't have to make coffee for yourself. We'll have servants for that."

"Servants that we'll pay with money from my trust fund?"

"It's a better use of it than paying for napkins and slutty pink t-shirts."

His snark and passive aggressiveness was impressive, especially since my pink t-shirts were *far* from slutty. Actually, he wasn't being passive at all. He outright said he was marrying me for my money. And my parents were all for it.

He was using money against me. Not just any money. *My* money.

I wasn't doing that again with Silas and the small business loan.

I was learning the very hard way from Cheney, but I wasn't falling for it twice.

No business with exes. What's the saying? *Don't shit where you eat.* How about, *Don't have sex where you want a business loan.*

I kept blaming Cheney, but he wasn't the only one I was angry with. My father was the one who made Cheney executor. He was pivotal... no, instrumental, in this whole mess.

They expected me to fall into line, to do with my life as they wanted. Nothing else. I was to become Cheney's wife and mother of his children. Nothing else. I could spend my money any way I wished as long as I made my parents–and Cheney–happy. They didn't care about my happiness. How had I made it all these years okay with this mess? I'd blindly gone along with what they'd wanted for me. Maybe it had been the distance of boarding school and college that had me missing all the signs. The cardigans and pearls shoved in the back of my closet were indication enough that I'd played along.

But I wasn't any longer. Still, it hurt. Parents were supposed to be supportive of a child's dreams, not make them take on theirs. They were forcing my hand and expected me to give in. The ultimatum was clear: My coffee shop or my family. I couldn't have both.

I chose the shop. I could make a family of my choosing instead of a family by blood.

I'd find some other way to get the money. Any which way.

But sex with Silas was happening. I was still sore from the day before. He was a thorough, vigorous and a beautifully rough lover. I'd come and come hard. He'd ensured I did and first. Who knew chivalry was dead? My pussy didn't.

I wasn't taking his money, but I could have his dick all I wanted. At the bar, he'd given it to me. At his office, he'd given it to me again. Then he texted last night and offered it once more and I'd missed it! The text and his dick. I never heard the notification.

I went to bed by eight. Eight, like a toddler or a coffee shop owner, only finding the message when I woke up.

> Next you'll be on top. I can watch your
> tits bounce as you ride me.

O.M.G. I squirmed and pretty much had a mini-orgasm as I read it, knowing Silas was just as eager. Thinking about me too. Wanting me. Pictured us together.

I wanted to be on top. As I watched Silas through my window, I imagined just that.

Him propped up in bed, me straddling his solid thighs and taking all of him into me. I'd have to hold on to his shoulders, push off for leverage because that dick was BIG.

Would it fit in that position?

Through his window, Silas picked up his cell. He began to pace... yes! Into the hallway so I could take in every sturdy, muscly, hard inch of him. Of what I could now have, anytime. Even before dawn?

I grabbed my cell. Texted a response.

> I'm game.

He paused—thank you baby Jesus–in the hallway and stared down at his phone. I watched as he typed on it. Not his fingers, but lower. Yeah, I stared at him *there.*

My phone pinged. He was texting me. Naked!

> I'm leaving in an hour for San Francisco.
> Now I'm hard. Fuck.

Yes, he was. I could actually see his dick getting harder. Because of me. He gripped it, gave it a long stroke. Holy shit, he was so turned on he had to ease the ache. I completely understood. He stopped and typed another text.

> When I come back next. You. Me. A
> bed. All night.

17

EVE

I WAS EMPTYING the filter from the large coffee brewer when the bell above the door jingled. In walked Frank, the mailman. He set my pile of mail–with probably a few bills–on the counter.

"Thanks!" I called as he turned and left, his letter bag slung over his shoulder. He offered a little wave as he shut the door behind him, moving to the architect firm next door.

Ignoring the filter and wet grounds, I flipped through the mail.

Bill. Bill. City flier for winter events. Bill.

"Fuck," I muttered.

June came over. "No luck with the bank loan?"

I shook my head. Frowned. "The three local banks won't give me one. I'm guessing it's my father. The owners all play golf with him. No doubt he told them to turn down my loan."

Nothing like the good ole' boys network fucking with me. Why wasn't my father my champion instead of my business nemesis?

She huffed, then practically growled, "That's totally wrong."

"It doesn't matter that your last name is Hunter and your family's loaded? That you are?"

I shook my head. "If my father's involved, then yes, but in his favor. Not mine."

"Maybe the bank doesn't know your assets are locked down by Asshole Ex. I didn't give him enough laxative."

I couldn't help but smile at her deviousness.

"They check things. Whatever they are. Or they listen to my dad. Either way, they said no. I'm still waiting to hear from the bigger bank in Missoula. That's a national chain, so maybe they won't be so stingy."

"Take Bridget up on their loan program."

I shook my head. "No. Absolutely not."

She tapped her finger on the counter.

"I may have an idea."

I turned to face her directly. "What is it?"

"Remember, I keep mentioning stripping?"

"I'm not stripping. My parents are losing their shit

over me and my little business. Can you imagine them finding out I'm stripping at the Pink Pony out by the highway?"

They'd have me committed.

"So what? You're an adult. There's nothing wrong with taking your clothes off for money."

I heard the hurt tone of her words. "You're right. I'm sorry. There's nothing wrong with it at all. But *me* stripping is the issue. I can't dance. I have zero rhythm and if there was a pole involved, I'd end up in the hospital with a head injury."

"That's true," she replied, tapping her lip. Her mouth turned up at the corners at the visual I made. "You can't even line dance."

"I can't. I really can't. Those women who strip, while I haven't seen any of them perform, have talent. They're gorgeous and skilled and... I can't keep up with their waxing regime."

"I wasn't suggesting the Pink Pony or waxing your body from the neck down."

Neck down?

I frowned, waiting for her to continue. She bit her lip.

"Out with it," I prodded.

"Ever wonder how I pay the bills between working here and ski patrol?"

"Are you saying you want a raise?" I asked.

She rolled her eyes and sighed. "I'm a cam girl."

I blinked. "What? I don't know what that is."

"I sorta strip. Online. In a chat room."

I stared at her. Blinked. "Um... what?"

She looked to the two moms who were chatting at a table while their toddlers napped in their strollers. They were too far away to pick up our conversation. Or interested. Then she peeked at the table by the window where Bridget and Mav were seated. Mav's dog was at his feet, asleep. Bridge must have sensed we were looking her way because she looked up from her laptop and glanced over.

She stood, making Mav glance from whatever papers he was reviewing. She grabbed their coffee mugs and gave him a kiss on the cheek before coming our way.

"Hey, you gave me a funny look," she said, glancing between us. "Something like, *rescue me now.*"

I bit my lip because June's secret was just that, *her* secret.

"I was telling Eve about being a cam girl," she shared.

So much for the secret.

"Oh, right," Bridget replied.

"You knew?" I asked her.

With a quick glance over her shoulder, it was clear Mav nor his dog cared about our conversation.

Bridget looked to June and shrugged. "Sure. We skied together a lot when I got back from MIT last winter."

As if that explained it all.

June nodded, then looked to me, continuing where we left off. "I set up a web cam in my bedroom and I do things viewers want. It's through a streaming site. Technically, it's live porn, but I'm alone and I don't have sex with anyone. The viewers make requests and donate money when I do what they ask for."

My mind was blown. June. *June* stripped in her bedroom.

"What kinds of things do the viewers want? Like sex stuff?"

She shrugged. "I take my clothes off and talk to them."

"Talk?"

Bridget filled one of the coffee mugs at the self-serve coffee urn on the counter and listened in.

"Yeah, sexy stuff," she added. "Asking them if they're hard, what gets them hot, asking them what I should take off first... Sometimes I sit there and fold laundry and–"

"You *fold laundry* and people watch? They pay extra for that?"

Bridget laughed, set the full cup on the counter and picked up the empty one. "Can you believe it?" She blushed, then offered a sly smile. "I think Mav would be all into me naked and doing laundry."

Huh.

"I'm in my bra and panties or naked or on the way to

naked and do it," June continued. "Or I paint my toenails. Or..."

"I get the idea. People pay for that?" Unbelievable.

She lit up. "Yes. A lot."

"I'm not a prude and I'm not knocking you for taking your clothes off, but that's not me. I don't think I could do that. Go naked."

I wasn't ashamed of my body. In fact, I considered it to be above average. But this was different.

I thought of Silas and how he walked around bare assed naked and imagined he wouldn't have an issue with it. Hell, he technically did his own cam show at five in the morning. Just for me. And he didn't know it.

Me? I liked being bent over a desk and ridden hard, but I wasn't so sure about naked in front of strangers from all over the world. Silas, sure, but randos? "I mean, I get up really early in the morning and sometimes I forget to shave my legs and—"

"You don't have to get naked," she clarified. "We could make up a persona for you. You could..."

"Make coffee?" I offered.

Bridget held up her hand. "Wait. You think you want to be a cam girl?" she asked. "Because you won't take the loan?"

I glanced away. "I can't take the money from Silas. I just can't."

She nodded. "I know and I understand. Streaming

live on a webcam is not a bad idea though. It's safe." She paused, bit her lip. "Well, reasonably safe if you don't get any crazy stalkers."

"What?" I asked, startled. "I don't want stalkers. I just want to make some money. Wait... what if someone recognizes me?"

June shrugged as if this wasn't a concern. "No one's recognized me yet and if they do, do you care?"

"My mother will," I countered, then realized what I said. "Yeah, okay. She'd lose her shit, but she loses her shit over my earring choices."

"Again, all of what you're freaking out about is why you go tame. You can do what you feel comfortable with and yeah, you could make brewing coffee look hot!"

June laughed. "That could work, but that'd be a lot of coffee to make. How about"–she looked me over as if inspecting me for sale–"oh! How about a virgin librarian!"

My brows went up and I stared at her wide eyed. Had I heard her correctly? "Excuse me?"

"If you think you'll be nervous on camera, then play that up. Be a virgin."

"I'm not a virgin," I said. A virgin didn't get fucked– and watched–in the back of a bar. Or on a conference room table.

"Be a *cam* virgin. Let them think you're sweet and innocent. Dress the part."

"Mav loves my glasses," Bridge said, leaning in and whispering. All three of us looked to Mav who was reading obliviously.

"It's the whole nerdy girl genius with the hot bod thing you have going on," June said, pointing up and down Bridget's body.

"What does a virgin wear specifically that screams *I haven't had sex?*" I asked.

"A cardigan. Pearls. Lacy bras and panties that are demure."

"You just described my mother," I grumbled.

"I'm just going to ignore you said that," June said. "I know you've got a shit-ton of cardigans your mom bought for you shoved way in the back of your closet and probably grandma's pearls in your jewelry box. We can find you a little plaid skirt at the thrift store and–"

I held up my hand. "I'm not doing schoolgirl stuff. That's... not okay with me."

Bridge nodded. "I agree. That's not you."

June hugged me, then stepped back, a little too happy.

"What?"

"You said you're not doing schoolgirl, which means you'll do something else."

I frowned at how she spun that around. "What kind of money are we talking here?"

She leaned close and told me an amount.

"A week?" Wow.

She shook her head.

"Oh, a month?" I asked, suddenly disappointed. That wasn't going to get me very far.

"A day."

"WHAT?"

"Wow," Bridget added, obviously overhearing.

June glanced at the moms again, then pulled me over to the pastry case. As if that would block our voices. Bridget came around the counter to join us, her coffees forgotten.

"I want to see this camming. Show me." I made grabby fingers and then held out my palm.

Pulling her cell from her jeans pocket, she swiped a bunch of times as I waited impatiently.

I was trying to get my head around the fact that my friend, that *June,* was a cam girl. A *naked* cam girl for money.

"I'm proud of you," I murmured.

She looked up from her swiping and gave me a sappy look. "Really?"

I nodded. "Yeah. You're doing your thing. I mean, I think every woman the world over would like to get paid that much money for doing her laundry."

"Well, here's my thing." She pushed the phone into my hands. "Push the start button. That's my free video. I turned the sound off."

Bridget stood beside me, her head close to mine to share the preview.

I turned the device sideways so the video was larger, then pressed play. There was June and... I angled my head keeping up with what she was doing with a laundry basket. Then the bits of clothing came off and I saw more of June than I ever had. I hit pause and handed the cell back. "Oh my. Totally proud. Your boobs look amazing."

"They really do. Wow," Bridget added.

June grinned. "If mine are nice, yours are going to bring in so much money. I mean, they're big and perky and–"

"I've seen them, thanks," I said, laughing. And blushing. Over talk about my boobs.

"Find a white or pink undies set. No, wait. Got any with cherries?"

Bridget snorted.

"You've got to be kidding me." *Cherries?*

June patted my shoulder. "I am. Sort of."

"I can't make that kind of money with clothes *on*. I mean, look at your body in that video." I pointed at her cell. "You're gorgeous. I can see why you make that kind of income, and doing laundry at the same time? You go, girl."

"You'll go on with me. I'll introduce you to my viewers. Once you get followers, they keep coming back."

"You could play a part," Bridge offered. "A role, then... oh! You'll read romance. Wait, make that erotica!"

They were getting way too into this. "What? Why?"

"Because then you don't have to think of sexy things to say. Reading it aloud gives you all kinds of naughty options. There's a never-ending supply of content."

That was true.

"I have to read it out loud?" I asked, staring wide-eyed at my friend.

Bridge rolled her eyes. "Not to yourself."

"Yes!" June added, getting into the idea. "We'll find the sexiest parts of books and you'll read them as you blush and talk about how the hero in the book's dick wouldn't be able to fit in your untried little pussy."

I stared at her wide eyed. "You've got to be kidding."

She set her hands on my shoulders, leaned down and got right in my face. "You had sex over the desk in the back office of a bar. With a stranger–"

Bridget laughed, then coughed. "Stranger? That was Silas. Oh my God."

"–while someone walked in and got an eyeful."

"Someone walked in?" Bridge gasped. "I didn't know about that."

I was really regretting sharing all that with June. "So?"

"So you have voyeur tendencies."

"Um, what?"

"Um, what?" Bridget parroted.

"Someone could have come into the office at any time," June reminded. "You knew that, and it got you hot. At least, I assume it did."

"It did." I started to think it was hot because I'd been with Silas. I felt safe with him. Uninhibited. Like the things that made me hot made him hot, too. While someone had seen us, Silas hadn't cared. I hadn't either.

"And you kept going. Someone actually did barge in, and you didn't freak. You kept right at it."

"God, I'm not going to be able to look him in the eye again for a while," Bridget murmured.

In that back office, Silas had his mouth on my pussy. I wouldn't have stopped if the fire department stormed in because he had been so good. He'd stopped mid-fuck to make sure I came by dropping to his knees and eating me out. His bare ass had been to the door so whomever came in had to have seen it. I wasn't mentioning any of that to Bridget.

"So I have voyeuristic tendencies." I shrugged.

"It's perfect for being a cam girl," June replied, completely unfazed by me having a kink. "And that embarrassed look you have on your face right now is perfect. You'll read something steamy and be mortified that it was actually possible. Guys will be watching and want to fuck you so hard. But you control it. You tease them. Lead them on. Work them for their money and give them just a peek."

"Fine. Fine!" I said, wanting to get her to stop pushing this as much as I wanted to make money. I was in trouble here and well this was an option. "I'll try it. *Try.* Clothes on. No laundry baskets."

"Oh my God, this is so cool," Bridget said. *She* wasn't the one taking her clothes off on the Internet. She stopped and looked me in the eye. "But what about Silas? I don't think your boyfriend will be too excited about this."

"He's not my anything." I said that and it made me a little depressed. True, but I had hope he'd come back soon and follow through with the me-on-top plan. "We had sex twice. Most of the time he's out of town."

"But he did say he wanted to see you again when he's back, right?" Bridget asked.

"Yes, he wants her to ride him like a cowgirl," June added.

"There was no mention of exclusivity. I'm a hookup when he's in town." And I liked watching him through my bedroom window in the mornings. "He doesn't live here."

"Tell that to Lindy," Bridget reminded. "Dex doesn't live here and now they're married."

"He *never* mentioned marriage," I clarified. Just

because he filled my thoughts didn't mean I expected forever.

"What if he did?"

"Marriage?" I questioned. "I barely know him."

"Fine. What about dating? What about if he was here and you could date. Get to know each other. The whole thing. Do you *like* him?"

I thought about it. Not for long because I knew the answer. "Yes, I *like* him. But it doesn't matter. He's in Japan or Jamaica or wherever. Guys, this isn't about Silas. I need money. You said this will be tame. I'll read erotica and wear cardigans, nothing more."

"Are you sure?" Bridget asked, suddenly doubtful after being so eager just a minute before.

"No, but it's worth a try. I can always stop, right?"

"Tonight," June prompted. "We're doing it tonight. Eight o'clock."

I was panicking. But the amount of money she mentioned? It was worth it. Except the time. "Eight? I'm in bed by eight."

"You're not in first grade. You can make it until nine. Besides, any longer and you'll panic and back out. I'll pick some good stories on my ereader. Come by and bring whatever you have that screams virgin librarian."

18

SILAS

"Excuse me, Mr. James," an employee said from the small opening she made in the conference room door. She glanced at all of us in turn apologetically for the interruption. Our meetings ran into the evening and they'd had dinner brought in.

Everyone at the table turned to look at her.

"Yes?" I asked.

"I'm sorry to interrupt, but your assistant asks that you check your phone for a message."

I offered her a small smile. "Thank you." I glanced at the three women and two men. "I apologize, please give me just a moment."

With a shift in my chair, I pulled my cell from my

pocket and swiped for a text. From Theo.

> How's your wrist from all that jerking
> off? Got carpal tunnel yet?

Such a dick brother thing to send, and he clearly hadn't gotten an update about fucking Eve in the conference room. It definitely wasn't why Bradley interrupted a meeting. There was another text. Bridget.

Instantly, a flare of worry surged through me. I was in San Francisco. Not near Hunter Valley if something was wrong. Until this exact moment, I hadn't really considered this challenge.

Fuck.

I swiped the text.

> Mav and I think you'd want to know
> about this. Let us know if we're wrong.
> Starts @ 8pm here, but not sure when
> that is for you.

I looked at the time on the phone. That was twenty minutes ago. Fuck! I pressed the link.

It pulled up a video and out came a loud female moan, followed by a… "Oh, that big dick is too big for my untried little pussy. It'll be too much!"

I blinked, then practically shouted, "What the fuck?"

Shit. Everyone in the room heard the woman's

breathy voice worried about taking too much and then my response.

Porn was the *last* thing I expected.

I fumbled with the volume on my cell. I felt like a middle schooler caught with a nudey magazine.

"What the hell was that?" someone asked. "Did I hear–"

I looked up, pasted on a fake smile that hopefully hid my total mortification. Shit. Shit!

"Absolutely not," I said quickly, shutting down the fact that they heard porn coming from my cell. In the middle of a meeting.

Thankfully, my beard hid the blush I could feel creeping across my cheeks.

"But–"

"One moment please." I spun my chair around to face away from the table. It was a snub, but fuck, what the hell did Bridget send?

With the phone held close to my chest, I looked at the video that was still running. Definitely an intro for porn.

A woman was on her bed in a red cardigan that was barely closed. Her breasts were practically busting open the remaining buttons, those lush globes filling out a pale pink lacy bra to perfection. Fuck, if she leaned in any further, her nipples might spill out.

Wait. WAIT!

That wasn't *any* woman. That was Eve.

What the actual fuck? Eve was doing porn? Live? RIGHT NOW?

I jumped to my feet, realized I had a hard on like a steel beam in my pants, then set my hands in front of it holding the phone. I spun about awkwardly, looked the vice president in the eye and hopefully keeping him from looking lower. I wasn't so sure about the rest of the Hyport group. "My apologies. There's something urgent I must see to on my phone."

I ducked out of the room and found the nearest empty office and slammed the door shut. Leaning against it, I tried to catch my breath as I studied the video again. With fumbling fingers, I turned the sound up, but only a little bit. Enough to hear what Eve was saying and no more.

"I'm not sure if I should read this story after all. It's really... ahem, naughty."

She looked up from what looked like an ereader and right into the camera. "You think I should?"

She bit her lip, unsure.

"Okay. Here goes. I've... I've never had a man touch me before. There. Oh, your finger feels so good. Is that why I'm all wet and sticky? It's all over my thighs, she explained to the lumberjack. His big cock was as big as his ax."

Lumberjack? Ax? It was a cam room and she was

dressed. She was alone, which meant she wasn't having sex with someone. She was streaming herself–in her bedroom?–reading porn. What would that be? Porn-adjacent?

Except porn-adjacent was still hot. I wasn't sure if I was losing brain cells by looking at her in that little sweater or if it was the pearls around her neck that made her seem so innocent and the words she was saying so fucking naughty.

"Oh, this story is actually really good. I didn't know I had a thing for lumberjacks. It's making me really hot. I think I need to undo my little sweater to try and cool off."

She glanced down at the remaining buttons, then up at the camera. Bit her lip.

"But does this make me a naughty little virgin letting you see more of my bra?"

I couldn't help it. My free hand fumbled with my leather belt, and I got it open and my fly down so I could grip my dick and stroke it as I watched Eve.

She was *not* a virgin. I knew exactly what those tits looked like and was well aware of how wet and sticky she got.

I stroked myself as I watched, completely mesmer-ized, as she popped one of those little buttons free and... fuck! While only an inch more of her pale skin was exposed, her tits looked incredible. They bounced when she took her little panting breaths.

In the corner was the word LIVE in vibrant red. She was doing this right now. *Now.* In Hunter Valley. I'd never been to her house before, but was that her bed? Beside the word was a count of how many people were watching. 473.

Almost five hundred horny fuckers–like me since I was jacking off to her sitting all prim and slutty on a bed–were seeing those lush tits and thinking about her virgin, swollen, sticky pussy.

Hell, to the fuck, NO.

"Oh, that's better. Where was I?"

She lifted the ereader and held it up as she read aloud.

"The burly man sucked his finger and licked all my pussy juices off. Climb on and take me for a ride. Good girl. I hovered over that club-sized head and tried to get it to fit. It won't go in... oh! It can't... I'm... you're opening up my little flower with that big meat."

Big meat? What the fuck was she reading?

"I can't take all of it. It hurts. My virgin pussy can't take– You'll take it all like a good girl."

A knock shook the door behind my back. "Is everything all right, Mr. James?"

I startled, gripped my dick harder at the interruption through the door.

"Remember good girls get their pussies fucked hard and deep. Oh, please!"

"What the hell?" I heard the person's concern, which meant he must be hearing the streaming, but it did nothing to stop my orgasm from seeing Eve's gorgeous cleavage and listening to her say such naughty, cum-inducing words. I came all over my hand when she whimpered the last. She was reading from a book. Some filthy, pervy erotic story. It was her voice, her breathy sounds that finished me, because I knew what they sounded like when it was real. When my dick was deep inside her. When she was saying that exact same thing when she looked up at me and told me she wanted it harder. Deeper.

"It hurts so good. Wait, I'm not on birth control so don't fill me with–"

The screen went black, then text came up. *YOUR FREE TIME IS UP. PLEASE PURCHASE THE MONTHLY SUBSCRIPTION TO CONTINUE.*

"Fuck!"

"Mr. James? Silas!"

"I'm fine," I pant-called. "Please give me a few more minutes."

I dropped my head back against the door. I was in an empty office at the Hyport US office building with my dick out, cum all over my hand, and Eve talking about getting railed for the first time by a lumberjack with a mega-dick and I got cut off by the porn service.

Pulling out a handkerchief–thanks to Bradley for

ensuring they were included with every suit packed for me–I wiped my hand semi-clean. Then I fumbled with the cell to purchase a membership to a cam site, not giving a shit that someone in accounting would see the expense on my corporate credit card bill. It took a few minutes of swiping and swearing, but I was back in with Eve.

I turned and leaned against the desk, relieved she was still there.

Now that I was a member, there was a box beneath LIVE that said private chat. I hit that faster than reasonable and paid more for private time with Eve. I couldn't join her now since I had to go back to the meeting and explain myself, but she was mine and mine alone.

No way were five hundred men going to ogle my woman.

No fucking way. Because with one flick of a cardigan button, Eve and her gorgeous body were all mine.

Mine.

19

EVE

I<small>T WAS</small> my fourth night as a cam girl and I was still getting the hang of it. That first night, I'd brought over a few outfit options and my grandmother's pearls, just like June expected. I'd joined her–she had on a sexy negligee–on her usual time slot. She'd introduced me as her BFF who wanted to talk to men but was too shy to do it in person. She shared a secret, that I was a virgin and had never seen a real dick.

I tried not to roll my eyes–or throw up from the nerves I felt–at her blatant lies. She'd asked the men watching if they'd share dick pics in the chat, which of course, they did. June fanned herself, looked to me and asked if I was hot from seeing all those gorgeous dicks. She continued by telling me I should undo a button on my cardigan to cool off. That night, it was a pale pink one.

I did. Then she asked, since I was a librarian, if I liked reading naughty books. I had to say I didn't know because I never read those kinds of stories before, because that was the basis for my entire... shtick. She asked her viewers if I should read some sexy scenes. Pop my erotic romance cherry. Again, they said yes. So I read a sex scene. I didn't have to fake being nervous or shy because I stumbled over myself. Then, I took a drink of water and dribbled it onto my cleavage, which it turned out they found hot as hell. Then it was over. But not before she told all her viewers to show up at my time slot an hour later.

I'd gotten through it thinking that Silas was watching, that I was saying every naughty thing and reading the sexy scene for him.

When I logged in on my own account, I discovered they did. They showed up en masse. And then again. Then again. It was absolutely insane, me trying hard to be sexy but messing up actually turned out to be a hit. I couldn't believe I had over four hundred people watching me read spicy scenes and undo buttons on my sweaters. Four hundred people translated into *a lot* of money. When June gave me a well-deserved *I told you so,* I caught on to why she did it.

Every night when I ended the call, I gave Cheney and my parents the mental middle finger.

Still, it was weird. It felt a little icky, but I was safe in my own bedroom. No one knew who I was. Where I lived. That I was only playing a role. In fact, it seemed they loved the part I played. So I caught on and started to work it. I read the hottest romances I could find with virgin heroines who seemed to have lived in a convent because they didn't know what a dick really did or how it could fit. It wasn't my favorite when it came to reading material, but I was savvy enough to grasp that men loved to be the one to break a woman in. Especially when the hero's dick was the size of a baby arm with balls filled with obscene quantities of cum.

Strange? Completely. But it did pay. And I kept my clothes on. Slightly unbuttoned, but still on. And kept sexy Silas in my mind as I read.

"With how she held her tits together, it was a snug fit around my dick. Her pussy too sore to fuck again so soon after breaking her in, but I had so much to show her. I couldn't last, ready to paint those fucking pouty lips of hers with my cum as her tits pressed tight around me. FUCK! I cried, watching as the head of my dick peeked out and I coated her neck and chin with thick ropes of it, draining my balls."

I put down the ereader and set my fingers on my pearls around my neck. Slid them back and forth. I bit my lip and looked at the laptop in front of me. "That hero really knows what he's doing. Is that what's called a pearl necklace?" I asked, all shy and hopefully looking a mix of confused and curious.

The screen went black. It had done that the night before, but no one had come on, only remained black for the duration of my cam time. Tonight, it had switched again. It was still a black screen, but the chat window had a name: CEOBill.

A private room. This guy, CEOBill, had bought my time and joined. From what June said, this was like a lap dance at a strip club or giving a private show in the back room. Extra money. Lots of it.

I frowned at the screen.

"Hi, CEOBill," I said. "Are you there?"

I waited, saw chat bubbles appear in the message area.

Yes. I can't show my face.

"Shy?" I asked, playing with my pearls again.

Yes.

"Me, too. I'm new to this. Talking on the computer. All of it."

I'm new too.

"Are you also a virgin?" I asked.

It was weird talking to a black screen, but he was paying.

Definitely not.

"Do you think I'd look good with the other kind of pearl necklace I read about? Think my breasts are big enough to be fucked?"

Painted in my cum? Fuck yes. Your tits are perfect.

I cocked my head to the side. "Are you hard thinking about it?" I ran my finger along my pearls again, then slid it lower through my cleavage and tugged open a button on my cardigan. "Oops."

Is that bra pink or lavender?

I glanced down and slid aside the sweater to reveal the lavender bra strap. "You like?"

Show me more.

Um... no. "I've never done that before."

Show a man your tits?

I nodded. On here, on camera, it was true.

I'm not any man and what you show me is just for me. There's no one else.

No one else. As if he's possessive and telling me no other men will ever see my body. I wasn't sure if I liked this after all. Four hundred strangers was a lot different than one guy probably fantasizing about getting his spunk all over my chest.

"Want me to read more of the story?" I asked, steering away from that topic.

Sure.

I picked up the ereader and found my place. I kept going for a few minutes, then looked up.

"The heroine gave him a blow job when she was on her knees and he was standing. Do you like it that way or is it better if you're in a chair or lying in bed?"

A guy will love a woman's mouth on his dick in any position.

I shook my head, cocked my head and gave him my slyest smile. "I asked you. Not any guy."

If it's your sexy mouth? I'd get you on your knees so you can look up at me as you take my dick as deep as you can. Another time we'd be in bed and we'd do sixty-nine. Know what that is?"

Yes, but I shook my head. I was a virgin librarian, after all. And I wanted to hear his answer.

It's when you sit on my face so I can lick your pussy while you suck me off.

I shook my head again and tried not to squirm. "Ooh, that's naughty getting my kitty licked like that."

I was making this up on the fly and had no idea what the hell I was saying. Kitty?

Glancing at the little timer in the corner, I said, "Your time is almost up. It was nice to meet you, CEOBill. I'll tell everyone during my time tomorrow night about how I learned about sixty-nine."

No, you won't.

I frowned. "They'll want to hear that I now know to sit on a man's face to get my kitty licked."

You'd come so hard, kitten, you'd scream my name.

Kitten? Oh my God. It was time to end this.

I gave him a little finger wave as the timer ran out. "Bye, Billy."

20

SILAS

"WHY THE HELL did you send me that link?" I asked Bridget. After washing my hands, then finishing up the meeting with the Hyport team–with tons of apologizing and disappointed looks–I'd gone directly back to my hotel room. In one of the Presidential Suites on the top floor since the Hyports were generous–and open to making me happy during negotiations.

"You saw it."

"Jesus, yes." I wasn't going to mention any more details than that. It had to have been my worst, and most embarrassing moments as CEO. While they hadn't said anything, I had no doubt the Hyport team knew I'd been watching something inappropriate. Watching Eve in almost-porn and probably seeing my epic hard-on during a meeting. Then I'd hid and jerked off in an empty office because my woman was reading X-rated sex scenes from romance novels and I was–like the other horny guys listening and watching–picturing all of it really happening to her.

Not with a lumberjack and his big ax, but with *me.* I knew what she looked like as she took my dick bent over a desk. The way her perfect ass jiggled with each thrust. Or the way she looked when she came as I loomed over her with her legs wrapped around waist.

I'd been in the worst situation ever.

That had been two days ago, and I'd bought up all her time. All of it. If she was talking with me, reading with *me*, unbuttoning the front of her little sweaters with ME, then she wasn't doing it for anyone else.

The next night, we'd talked–thank fuck in private and nowhere anyone from Hyport would hear–about blow jobs and sixty-nine. I'd had to end our evening meetings early, but it was worth it. Just thinking about it now and I was hard again. I had to stand because sitting was uncomfortable.

"Well?" she prodded.

"Well, what?" I paced, ran a hand through my hair. Wished I had a Danish spandauer right about now.

"What are you going to do about it?" she asked.

I couldn't go into Steaming Hotties and tell Eve to

shut that shit down and force money on her. For one, I was in San Francisco. Two, I didn't want to be throat punched. I wanted my dick down her throat. There was a very clear distinction, and it was my actions that determined which one I received.

"She's a cam girl. What can I do about it?" I wanted to fly back to Hunter Valley and tell her the only one she could do something like that with was me. Not throat punching, but... anything sexy.

I remembered the conversation with Dex when he talked about video calls and doing sex stuff with Lindy. Where had I been? Right, Denmark. Now I saw why he was all over the concept. I'd just done it... twice with Eve and it had been H.O.T.

I'd gotten hard in a roomful of Hyport hoteliers, for fuck's sake.

"I talked to Mav about it, and we felt you needed to know this is what she's doing for money to keep Steaming Hotties going," she explained. "Not that there's anything wrong with it because it's empower–"

I froze in my pacing. "What?"

"It's empowering, and she's a marketing and branding genius with her idea of being a naughty librar–"

"Not that," I interrupted, swiping my hand through the air. "The other part."

"The other... oh. She's done it for a few days, and she said the money's good. Like really good."

"She's camming, or whatever the hell it's called, because she wouldn't take the James Corp small business loan?" I asked, stunned.

"Yes," she replied simply.

I ran a hand through my hair. This was my fault then because we slept together. Because I couldn't keep my hands off her. Because I had to drag her to the back office at a bar or push her back on the conference room table. Shit.

She was camming because of me. Was this what women who'd been under my father's thrall been forced to do? Had their livelihoods been so impacted by him using them for a quick fuck that they had to play a virgin librarian to pay their bills?

Fuck me. I'd solve this.

"I've already booked out her sessions," I told her. No way is another guy seeing her like that. Those perfect tits. That voice. The way she bit her lip. Even talking about sixty-nine or BJs or anything remotely sexual and guys were going to blow their load.

"What's that mean?"

Obviously she didn't know much about this type of thing. Not that I did either. Not until she sent me the link. "You can pay for a private room with her. I did that and I set it for the rest of this week." I paused. A week.

That wasn't long enough. Fuck. It would take a few months for her to earn what was being offered in the loan. "Wait. That's not long enough. I'll change that to the rest of the month."

She was quiet for a moment. For Bridget, that meant that she was thinking, which she did a hell of a lot.

"So you're going to what... visit her every night and monopolize her cam time yourself?"

Yes. Exactly that. "Abso-fucking-lutely."

"You like her."

Fuck, I admired Eve for this... ingenuity, for finding a way to get money for her business, but this? I hadn't expected it. Holy hell, never in a million years.

"Yes."

Bridget knew all too well we had a fling. Twice. Knew I didn't think our flings should hold Eve and her business success back. Now Bridget was learning that Eve meant something. So I told her the truth. "I don't want anyone else to see her like that."

Except for the person who walked in on us at the bar, whoever the hell it was. But that didn't matter because it had been *my* mouth on her pussy. My name she screamed. The fucker knew she was taken and being well taken care of. By me. I didn't give a shit if the guy got an eyeful. Whatever, because Eve knew when I made her come she was mine.

Until she walked out. Thanked me for the orgasms

and went on her way. Then turned down the James Corp loan. Because of sex. With me.

"So, she won't take money from you because you had sex, but you're going to give her the money to keep her business afloat this way instead."

That about summed it up.

"Looks like it."

"Wait." She paused and I could see her pushing up her glasses as she thought. "Wait. She doesn't know it's you on there, does she?"

Bridget was ridiculously smart. I didn't say anything.

"Oh my God. She doesn't know. Sil–"

"If I tell her, she'll block me or whatever. I don't want other men seeing her. No way. If this is the only way to give her that money, then so be it."

"You know who she is, don't you? Her family?"

"Um, yeah. Eve. Evelyn."

"Right. Evelyn *Hunter*."

I wasn't following. "So?"

"Hunter, as in Hunter Valley."

What? "The town is named after her family?"

"I forget you're not from here. No, her family practically owns the valley."

"*You* forgot?" Impossible. She probably remembered what shoes she wore to her first day of kindergarten.

"Her great, great, great something founded the town.

It was her grandparents who created the resort and where the real money came in."

"So her parents run it?" I needed to look into that company.

"No. Her aunt. Her son, Eve's cousin, is named Hunter. He's the town sheriff."

Strange, but whatever.

"Okay, so what about her parents?"

"They don't work."

"Because of the family money?" I asked.

"Because of the family money," she repeated. "I've known Eve since we were kids. Her parents stay up on the mountain. Live the posh lifestyle wholeheartedly. I met them once. I was maybe... eleven. Eve and I were in 4H and helping out with the show chickens."

"What the hell is a show chicken?" I grew up in Denver. A big city. I ate chicken. The only ones I came across were on my plate or under plastic at the grocery store. Which I never went to because I was never fucking home.

"They're entered into contests at the county fair. They're judged and ribbons are handed out. Not just chickens. Rabbits. Cows. All the animals."

"What does this have to do with Eve?"

She sighed. "Her parents found out she was having fun. With chickens. Yup. It was actually fun and it's an interesting area of science–"

I dropped back onto the couch, my hard on gone after the talk about fowl. "Okay, focus please."

"They yanked her from 4H and shipped her to boarding school."

I flopped back, stared at the ceiling. "Oh. That kind of parents."

I knew them all too well. I grew up with families like that, where kids were ignored and shipped off to school. Or pranced about like show ponies.

Or, in Eve's case, probably both. No Hunter would get her hands dirty in a pole barn and the only way to ensure that was to move. God forbid the parents up and relocated. No, she ended up in some far-flung school for rich kids with shitty families.

"Now do you see?"

"No."

"She has money. Or her family does. Yet she applied to James Corp for one of the local loans."

"Okay." I was trying to figure out where she was going with this.

"Silas, don't you see?"

"Obviously not."

"She refused the James Corp loan out of fear of being financially controlled by a man she had sex with."

"Are you saying this is a trend, or just me?" I wondered. I didn't want to think of her having sex with her ex, or him controlling her somehow with money, but that would be hypocritical. If this was the case, he was old news. I was the one who was fucking her and fucking her well.

I wouldn't control her with money. No way.

"I don't know, but you were there. She was adamant."

"And I accepted that, but you said *she had sex with.* We're having sex," I clarified. "I might be in San Francisco, but it's definitely not past tense. When I get back to town–"

"Whatever." I had a feeling she waved her hand through the air. "My point is, now you're financially controlling her again, but this time *without her knowing it's you.* This is exactly what she doesn't want."

"Too bad. There is no way in hell I'm letting other men see her like this. And we both know–you and me– that I wouldn't fuck with that loan. This is only a different way for me to give her the money. This time, no interest, no paying it back."

"But there is still a cost, Silas."

"No there isn't," I countered. "It's me. We've had sex. There's nothing different about what we did and what we're doing in a cam room except the actual sex part."

"TMI," she grumbled. "She's camming. That's her cost. It goes to show how determined she is not to take the loan from us. And how much she needs one."

"She's camming for me. Me. CEOBill. Not a stranger."

"CEOBill?"

"My screen name."

"Well, in that room, you are a stranger to her. She doesn't know it's you!" She sighed. "Silas. You *like* her. How are you going to take her out on a date or whatever without telling her you know?"

"I can't tell her I know."

"She needs to know it's you. You have to tell her."

"There's no way she can know I know. She won't take the money, and like you said, she needs it. Me knowing is enough."

"Well, I know that you know, and she doesn't know that you know. I can't look her in the eye knowing that she doesn't know when I know that you know. What am I supposed to do?"

This was getting ridiculous and really hard to follow. "Don't do anything. I'll be back in a week. I'll take care of it."

"No. Today. You have to call her and tell her it's you in that room, today."

"Fine."

I'd tell her today. If I only knew how.

21

EVE

CEOBILL WAS BACK. Not just back, but he'd booked all my time. For the rest of the month.

"Hi, Billy. You must really like romance books to want to talk with a naughty librarian every night," I said, looking at his black screen on my laptop. The computer was on my bed in front of me, as usual.

I'm greedy. I want you to be naughty only for me.

I wasn't sure if I liked the idea of that, of talking only with him, whoever he was. Showing myself to hundreds of men at once, even if I did flash them a little cleavage, was less intimate and the last thing I wanted was to get personal with a guy in a cam room.

"I'm not *that* naughty," I reminded. "I'm not ready yet

to do too much. I mean, the things I read aloud... I don't think I could do them."

You could do them all, with the right person.

"Like you?" I asked, sliding my finger back and forth along my pearl necklace.

Like me. Whatever you need, I'd give you. Whatever your fantasy, I'd fulfill.

And that was it. This was creepy.

"Sorry Billy, I, um... I just realized I can't stay on. Gotta go."

I hit the End Call button and shut the private room down.

I flopped back on my bed, stared at the ceiling.

June might be able to do this, but I couldn't. I had to hope the bank in Missoula would come through.

22

EVE

"Good, you're here too," I said, approaching the counter, and Bridget. It would make this conversation a lot easier since she and June were together. The shop was quiet, and I'd been able to duck out and go to Van's, the local grocery store, to pick up a ten-pound bag of sugar. June was behind the counter and Bridget was putting milk in her to-go cup. She wore a knit hat with a big pom-pom on top. Combined that with her glasses and she looked sixteen.

"I wanted to tell you about the camming."

"We were just talking about that," June said, wiping down the counter. "She wants to know specifically how it's going. Tell her how you have so many followers. We want an update."

I shook my head. "I stopped. Last night."

June's eyes widened. "Stopped? Why? You were raking in the cash."

"Because I got one guy in a private room, and he was talking about giving me whatever I need and coming all over me and..." I shivered. "How come stuff like that is super-hot to read and hot to do with a guy in real life, but in a cam room, I'm all squidged out?"

June's eyes widened. "Because you don't know anything about him," she reminded. "Where he lives. I don't think they can do cam stuff in prison, but he could be an ax murderer."

I laughed but her words didn't help me feel any less creeped out. Could he really be in prison?

"I did a private room once," she said. "I know what you mean. I'd rather be in front of a few hundred horny guys sharing dick pics in the comments over one."

"Has he told you anything about himself?" Bridget asked, taking a sip of her drink.

"Some things," I replied. There was a stray straw wrapper on the floor, and I grabbed it. "He has a big dick–"

"You've *seen* it?" Bridget's eyes widened behind her glasses.

I shook my head. "Well, no, but he told me about it, how I make him hard."

She frowned, like the sip she took of her coffee had bad milk.

"Gross."

"I'm glad you stopped," June told me. "At least the private room. I don't think there's enough red flags in existence to cover a guy getting too into you in there. We grew up knowing not to connect with strangers on the Internet. Fall for them or whatever they might be saying. Ever heard of sex trafficking? Or worse, he could be grooming you for a Satanic sex ritual!"

"That's a little over the top," I admitted, but agreed she could be right. "I talked to him the first time. Then he got on again last night and I cut it short after only a few minutes. He wasn't gross or anything, but a black screen and all made it weird. Then again, seeing the guy jerking off or whatever might be a hell of a lot weirder. Plus, your talk about cults and sex trafficking are only freaking me out even more." I looked to June. "Why didn't you start with those possibilities when you had me start camming?"

"Wait, he went on a second time?" Bridget asked, steering back to Billy and the private chat.

I nodded, then waved goodbye to two older men who stopped by almost every morning. "Yes. He bought my

time for the *month*. Can you believe that? Do you think
he's a stalker?"

"God, maybe. Skip private chats," June suggested.
"Do the group thing like you started out and don't accept
any privates."

I shook my head. "No. Groups or not, I don't think
camming is for me. I just... can't. I'm waiting to hear from
the bank in Missoula about the loan. I have enough money
to float for a little while. I can hold on a little bit longer."

"What about Silas?" Bridget asked.

"Yeah, what about Silas?" June asked. "He's real and
isn't in a cult. He fucks you on tables and desks. He
makes you come. He's got a big dick. Please say he has a
huge dick."

I thought about it, seeing it across our backyards,
then up close in the conference room. Then feeling how
impressive it was deep inside me. "He does. The last time
he texted, he was in California. He might be real, but he's
definitely not here."

"He's coming back though," June added. "You told
me you made plans for having in-bed sex when he
returned."

"What does Silas have to do with anything? I mean, I
turned down the James Corp loan and when he comes
back to town, we'll hopefully have more sex and we can
see if it goes somewhere."

"I'm going to kill him." Bridget swore, setting her cup down then resting her hands on her hips. She looked fierce all of a sudden.

June and I eyed her.

"Who? Silas? Why?" I wondered. "Because we had sex on your conference table? I'd say I was sorry about that, but I'm kinda not."

"No. Because he's your stalker. He's CEOBill."

I stared at her. Processed. Then processed a little more. "Wait. How did you know that name?"

"Because he told me."

"Who?"

"Silas."

I blinked because *what?* "What... are you saying–Silas is Billy, the guy in the private cam room?"

She nodded. "CEOBill is–"

"CEO billionaire," June said, catching on.

Bridget kept right on bobbing her head. "I was the one who told him you took up camming."

I was sure my cheeks were a bright red because they were hot. It was supposed to be a secret. Anonymous. "Oh my God. Why?"

"Because you're doing it because of him. Because it was an alternative to taking the James Corp loan. Because you guys had sex."

"So?"

"You wouldn't have turned down the loan if you hadn't slept with him."

"So?"

"So, why do you have to go on camera and do slutty stuff–no offense, June–because you two slept together? It's his fault you couldn't take the loan. I told him about your streaming because it was a way for him to make things right. You need the money."

"Not that badly, I don't," I replied. "Bridget, this is worse than taking the loan. Before, it was one-time, anonymous sex. Now it's me doing sexy stuff while he watches and pays. This is far worse."

"I know. I thought about it after we talked. It's not fair he gets orgasms with zero consequences. Meanwhile, you have sex and you could lose your business."

June held up her hand. "Wait. Silas booked the private room so he could give her money that way? Instead of the loan?"

Bridget nodded.

"Holy shit," I whispered. So Billy wasn't a creeper, but he was Silas. "That little sneak. It's the exact same thing. It's still about sex and money."

Bridget shook her head. "I didn't tell him to go and buy out your time in a private chat room. I told him to tell you he knows about the camming, that he's CEOBill and to... help you find another solution. I gave him a day and he obviously didn't do it."

I went around the counter, started to make a fresh pot of coffee to keep busy while I worked through this new info.

"Eve?" June asked, her voice soft. She gave me room, let me putter.

"I'm thinking."

Silas wanted to give me money to wear too small cardigans and read about lumberjacks fucking virgins.

I spun around, leaned against the counter as I held the huge coffee ground holder. "He's actually, in a ridiculous way, being a nice guy. He's giving me the money and hijacking the cam time so it's only the two of us."

"Yeah, if he wasn't an idiot, it'd be sweet," Bridget added.

"He's being possessive, doing a private room and then booking you all month," June added. "That's really hot."

I smiled. Silas, the idiot. Thinking back to the stuff we talked about without the creepy factor, it was now a turn on. Knowing the stuff that CEOBill wrote and it being Silas, it made sense. It was clearly Silas's kind of sexy. I'd been aroused and not knowing who it was had me shutting it down. But with Silas? Totally hot. Totally different perspective.

"He doesn't know that I know?" I asked Bridget.

She shook her head. Grabbing her drink, she took a tentative sip.

"Good. Don't tell him," I said, looking her in the eye and smiling.

June held up her hand and took the coffee maker part from me. "I know that look. What are you thinking?"

"Let Silas keep up his secret identity." He wanted me to undo buttons on my cardigan? Show him my panties? Oh, I'd show him. I'd show him *everything*.

"But it's not a secret."

"He doesn't know that," I said, cocking my hip against the counter.

June's eyes widened, then she slowly grinned. "Payback's a bitch."

Bridget blinked. "I don't understand."

"I know he knows about me camming. But he doesn't know I know. Right?"

"Right," she said slowly, clearly unsure where I was going with this.

"It's time to have a little fun. He wants to watch a virgin librarian undo buttons on her cardigan while she reads about a woman being railed by triplets, then I'll give it to him. As for actual payback... the money he's giving me? I'm giving it to the animal shelter."

23

SILAS

"Sorry I had to leave early yesterday," she said. She sat coyly on her bed in a black skirt and a green cardigan. It was so tight that if she took a deep breath or raised her arms over her head, the buttons would pop. Her cleavage was pale and creamy hoisted by a bra that was edged in purple lace. They were right fucking there... on the screen.

Fuck, I wanted to touch her. Fuck her. Make her come.

I realized she was waiting for me to respond, so I typed, *Are you all right?*

She nodded. Her long hair was pulled up into some tangled updo with strands framing her face. One slid across her cheek and she brushed it away. "Yes, and I'm back now. Did you miss me?"

Did I miss her?

I shifted in my desk chair because my dick was hard. That didn't work so I moved again, unzipped my pants and let my dick out to play. I ended meetings early and went into the office Hyport gave me to use and locked the door. No one could see me, unless they were in a helicopter hovering outside the thirty-fourth floor of the skyscraper.

I stroked it in a firm grip from root to tip, then realized she was waiting for an answer. I couldn't get off and type at the same time.

My dick's been hard all day waiting for you.

It had. I wondered why she cut the call short the night before, if she was okay. I'd wanted to text her, but I went back to the late meetings. By the time I was able to, it was late and assumed she was asleep.

I watched her throat work as she swallowed, then glanced away. I couldn't miss the blush on her cheeks. Was she suddenly shy? Was it still a virginal act or did she like this dirty talk?

You look amazing in green.

She glanced down at her prim sweater. Her attire, while sexy as hell, was stuffy and conservative. It wasn't what Eve normally wore. Her personality and clothing were more carefree.

"Thanks." She ran her fingers down the taut front. "I can't seem to keep the buttons closed." A button popped free with a little help from her fingers. "Oops."

Oops? One more and those full tits would spill out. I never hoped for weak thread before in my life.

What are you going to read for me tonight?

She picked up her ereader and shared three titles. I couldn't miss the way she leaned slightly forward.

"One has a heroine who was naughty and is taken over the hero's knee for a spanking. I think it also involves a plug in her bottom, which is so, so..." She sighed as if unsure of what she thought about that.

I'd touched that tight ass of hers and she'd come from the lightest brush of my thumb. She might be playing at being a virgin, but that hole? Untried.

I wasn't sure if I could survive listening to her read about getting her ass plugged. I had to grip the base of my dick in a tight hold to stave off coming.

What else?

"A virgin is fucked for the first time by the college quarterback and a few of his teammates catch them and watch."

And the last?

"She's sold at a virgin auction at a brothel in an Old West saloon." Her gaze shifted from her ereader to the laptop. To me. "Which one would you like?"

Like? I want to know what makes your little panties all wet. Are you wearing panties?

She gasped, as if the idea of going without them was unfathomable. "Of course!"

Show me.

Come on, Eve. Show me your fucking panties, I thought to myself.

She swallowed again. "Um, my panties? Here? Now? Billy, I don't show strangers my panties."

I was far from a fucking stranger. I knew how she tasted. How she screamed when she came. How she–

Pre-cum spurted from my dick as I typed with frustration.

I'm not a stranger.

"You are. I don't know anything about you. I can't even see what you look like."

If she saw me, she'd somehow kill me through the laptop.

I'm six-two. Fair hair. I have a mole on my right butt cheek.

She laughed. "You share your mole?"

Do you want me to talk about my dick?

It was throbbing right now.

She licked my lips. "God, yes. Is it hard?"

For you, kitten, always.

"Oh," she said, her voice going soft.

If you won't show me how wet your panties are with them on, take them off and hold them up.

"Hold them up?"

Hell yeah. Smartest idea I had all day.

She thought for a moment. "Okay, but that will cost you," she replied.

What?

"I only do naughty things for extra money. Use the Donate button. It's the little red heart in the corner." She ran her finger along the swell of one breast, then flicked a button open, giving me even more of a tease.

I blinked. Fuck, she was practically hypnotizing me with her cleavage. I saw the heart. She wanted me to give her *more* money? My dick was telling me to push the fucking button, so I did.

"Thanks, Billy," she said, then cocked her head and smiled. "I'll show you my panties."

I was transfixed as she went up on her knees and slid her hands up the outside of her thighs beneath her skirt. Then she wiggled and tugged the dainty scrap down. I didn't see her pussy because her skirt covered it. Dropping to her butt on the bed, she lifted her legs and slid the panties off her bare feet.

She shifted to kneel in front of the camera again, the lacy scrap in her fist.

Show me.

She grinned, raised her hand so I could only see a

hint of the material in her clenched fist. I imagined she could smell her arousal.

I knew exactly that scent and I growled, not that she could hear.

She shook her head and pointed to the lower corner where the donate heart was.

I sent her more money.

After a few seconds, she let the pink lace dangle from her fingers.

Show me the wet spot. I know it's there.

She shook her head, pointed at the corner of the screen again.

You want more money?

"You want to see how wet I really am?"

Fuck. Fuck! While she was in Hunter Valley, hundreds of miles away, she had me by the balls. I pushed the Donate button and sent her more.

A second or two later, she grinned. Turning the panties around, she held them closer to the camera so I could see the darkened fabric at the gusset.

Holy shit, she was wet. From talking with a stranger on an Internet cam private room.

I grabbed my phone. Texted her. Because she needed to hear from me. Silas. Not Billy. I was the one whose dick she actually was going to get.

> I can't wait to get back to Hunter Valley and have you ride my dick.

Instead of texting, I should just turn on the camera on my laptop and show her my face. Let her know I was Billy. Bridget was adamant I do it. I agreed with her it was the right thing to do, but this? With Eve? She showed me the fucking wet spot on her panties. I couldn't tell her who I really was now.

"See? My pussy is wet."

Holy fuck. My fingers fumbled over the keyboard.

Wet at the idea of the teammates watching the heroine get fucked, right?

Eve liked to be watched. I had no doubt that was what was making her squirm right now. I loved knowing this, loved that she wasn't the shy virgin, but the uninhibited woman who knew what got her hot. This entire cam room fed into her kink.

And mine because I was going to listen to her and jerk off. She'd reduced me to a horny teenager.

"Yes."

Read it to me.

24

SILAS

"SILAS." Robert Hyport, the company's CEO and founder, called to me as I stood in front of the bank of elevators. A ding announced the arrival of one of the cars, but I ignored it and turned to face the older man.

"May we talk in my office?" he asked.

Our meetings were scheduled in the evenings, rather than during the day. A little unorthodox, but everyone involved in the upcoming merger had the day-to-day running of our two corporations to also handle on top of the negotiations.

He held out his arm indicating I should precede him down the hall. For some reason, I felt like I was headed to the principal's office for a scolding. I hadn't been in the mood for one when I was a kid and whatever he wanted to talk about could probably wait.

I was going to be late for my cam time with Eve and that took precedence over everything.

He closed the door behind me and went around his desk. "Please sit."

I did. I knew, as CEO, that one could learn more from keeping quiet. Maybe I learned that back in middle school and Principal Shemanski. Now she'd been a ball buster.

"I see that the meetings are ending early for the third night this week."

I nodded. "Yes. We're starting at three instead of four to compensate. I now have a consistent meeting at seven." With Eve in the cam room.

It might be eight in Hunter Valley, but I was an hour behind.

"Meeting or porn addiction?"

Shit. Shit!

I wanted to freak out, but I wasn't going to show my hand. I hadn't yet in any of the merger talks and I wasn't going to now with this. Although there was a big difference between negotiating a billion-dollar deal and trying to talk my way out of watching porn. "Excuse me?"

"The porn that you pulled up during the meeting and I assume you're watching every night at seven."

What I did with Eve in the cam room might be

considered porn to him, but it wasn't. Not to me. It was me and my woman having fun. There was zero wrong with that. Except that I'd been caught.

"That was—"

He held up his hand to stop me.

"I've dealt with your father," he said, his voice more disappointed than angry. "I knew what he was up to with my secretary and the strip clubs. That was why the sale with him didn't go through all those years ago. The deal made sense then and it makes more sense now. I want to retire and while my son wants to take over, it's not his dream. Selling will let my legacy live on and ensure financial stability for generations of Hyports to come."

Stability? The merger was in the billion-dollar range. That was really fucking stable.

He was in his late sixties, a similar age to what my father would be now, if he lived. He knew as much, or if not more, about how my father's extracurricular activities affected his work.

I had no interest in his current assistant, especially since he was a man, but I wouldn't have gone there anyway. The only woman I wanted was Eve.

Thus, the cam time and my obsession with her.

"Mr. Hyport, I assure you—"

With a quick shake of his head, he said, "Don't. I heard it with him, and you assured me things were different. That his... behavior died with him."

I heard the disappointment in his voice.

"It did," I vowed. "I'm nothing like my father. Nothing."

I was making that crystal clear with him, even though he'd believed in me enough to begin a new round of sale negotiations now. With me. The new era of James Corp.

"Then explain to me the porn that you pulled up on your phone." His voice didn't go up but got quieter. Not a good sign. "And your disappearance into your office every night instead of finalizing the merger. I expected more from you. Perhaps you're only more subtle in your behavior than your father was."

I swallowed. Shit. SHIT!

Any therapist would say everyone had a trigger, something that poked at a festering, unresolved wound from childhood. Mine? Being anything like my father. Hyport was outright saying we were *like father, like son* when it was absolutely, completely not the truth.

I did everything, *everything,* to distance myself from the man and his behavior.

Now, the deal was going to go south because I actually was behaving just like the guy. Fucking a woman and then playing games with her in a cam room. If there had been live streaming in my father's day, I had no doubt he'd have lost a fortune with all the women bleeding him dry for showing off her panties or doing raunchier things.

The only difference was that I wanted Eve. Wanted more from her than a quick fuck or two. Or some sexy fun in a cam room. I was doing it because I was possessive, but I also wanted to give her the money for Steaming Hotties that she wouldn't accept with the loan.

I wanted all of her, but the merger was the deal of my career.

Fuck!

Hyport was a family man. Married for decades with five grown kids. One of them was the VP.

This deal was over unless I came up with something and something good. Right now.

I'd been caught. I couldn't tell him what he overheard wasn't porn. Especially when they all heard the voice of a woman who said something about a big dick was too much for her virgin pussy. I also left early each night at the same time as the original porn-watching fiasco to go in the chat room. And to jerk off watching her.

He waited.

"It wasn't porn. It was my wife."

He blinked and his mouth parted. I'd stunned him. Not just with the words, but with my tone. No one told me what I did with Eve was wrong.

"Wife?" he asked eventually.

I nodded. Fuck, it was the only spontaneous thing I could think of that would work. He wasn't going to accept me, a single man, watching porn. As if I had to go on the Internet and find nasty shit to get off. Not after my father. While I doubted my father fucked the assistant during a meeting, I'd actually–and unintentionally–opened a porn site with the Hyport team in the conference room.

Robert wouldn't be thrilled if I said it had been a girlfriend. That term made it sound like I was in high school, not thirty-four years old. And doing sexy shit with a girlfriend wouldn't play with him. With five grown children, he probably knew people had sex before marriage, but with my father's history, he wanted to deal with a guy who was pretty much a monk.

I didn't blame Robert for any of this. He was right to question and if the roles were reversed, I wouldn't do the deal with him either. But I wasn't my father.

Therefore, I had to lie. It had to be a wife.

"Yes, we married two months ago."

A smile spread across his face, and I could see the tension releasing from his body. "I hadn't heard. No one has, as far as I know."

He glanced at my left hand which rested on my thigh, searching for a ring.

I shook my head. "It's been a secret. It was a whirl-wind romance, really."

"I knew Mrs. Hyport was the one for me five minutes into our first date," he admitted.

"Love at first sight."

He nodded.

"I'm sure you saw one of those gossip magazines put me as their top eligible bachelors," I added.

He nodded. It wasn't part of my CV as CEO, but social media circles cast me as an epic catch for a woman. I wasn't hard on the eyes and had a huge bank account.

"I wanted to have some time, at least for a little while, with her all to myself before the media learned about it. She's not used to any kind of spotlight." I paused and actually blushed remembering how I'd gotten hard in the middle of the meeting when I pulled up Eve's live stream. "I admit, the link she sent me was..." I cleared my throat. "...a little inappropriate, and for that I apologize. It wasn't a random woman on there. It was her. I'm traveling all the time for this deal. Denmark, Singapore, all over. Well, you know what being a newlywed is like."

God, I really fucking hope he did.

He grinned. "We didn't have cell phones back in my day but when I got home..."

"Right. Right." I scrubbed at the back of my neck, hoping I looked a little contrite and embarrassed at being caught out. "She, um... runs a coffee shop and seven is the only time we can connect. She goes to sleep early."

Now it wasn't any random woman, my imaginary wife was now Eve.

"I see."

"She called me and obviously expected me to be alone. But I wasn't and I definitely didn't expect her to surprise me in such a... private way. Again, apologies."

"You're ducking out early every night to talk with her?"

"Yes, sir." That wasn't a lie. I was doing exactly that. Just with her on camera in barely-there sweaters and pearls. "As I said, I've adjusted the schedule earlier so our meetings won't be cut short. But my wife... it's important I–"

"I understand." He stood and came around the desk.

I hopped to my feet and took my first deep breath in the past five minutes.

"Congratulations then. I shall keep your secret."

I smiled. Genuinely. Because holy fuck, was that close.

"Please give your wife my best when you talk. In private."

I nodded, then left, making my way back to the elevators.

Two things came to mind. One, that was fucking

close. Two, no way in hell was I telling my sexy virgin librarian the CEO of Hyport wishes us best in our marriage.

25

EVE

I REPLIED to Silas's text, the one he'd sent while we were in the cam room. The one that meant he was as horny as I was while we chatted. The fact that he'd paid a few hundred dollars extra to see me take off my panties was proof. Then another few hundred to see the wet spot. I realized the power I had over him. I knew how much he wanted me.

I wasn't unaffected. What we talked about, what I read aloud to him? We'd never have jumped to that level of connection if it wasn't in the cam room. It gave us freedom to admit things. To do things I would never have imagined with a guy I barely knew. Sure, we'd had hot sex twice, but this? It was a whole new level of kinky.

I was calling him by a completely different name, which was pretty hard to remember to do.

The whole crazy thing was like foreplay. Mean, unrequited foreplay since we weren't in the same state. We couldn't fuck like rabbits to take the edge off.

Even through all that, the panty strip tease, the rest of the call, he hadn't outed himself. Why? I had no idea.

I did know that when we got together–in person–it was going to be insane. I was going to climb him like a monkey. I typed my reply:

I'm wet. I'm ready.

I was. I so was. Camming for Silas was so naughty... and ridiculously lucrative. I had Silas by the wallet and the balls. Except I'd never been so horny in my life, and I had a feeling it was going to get a whole lot worse.

26

SILAS

You've worn green three nights in a row. Is it your favorite color?

"No," she said, playing with the neckline, this one the color of grass. "My favorite color is pink."

"Holy shit," I said to myself. Even though Robert had scolded me, and I felt like shit about it, I couldn't stop with Eve. This was our time. Our secret space. It wasn't a porn addiction like he'd mentioned. It was an *Eve* addiction.

I needed this time with her. If I couldn't be in Hunter Valley with her, I would take this.

Pink? Like your pussy? Are those glossy, swollen lips pale or a dusky rose?

I knew the answer, especially the pretty pink shade of her pussy. I'd had an up close and *very* personal view as I licked and fingered her to orgasm. How it took my dick so well.

"Oh... um, dusky."

Do your nipples match?

I knew that, too. I'd cupped them, felt their weight.

"Billy," she said, her voice a little whimper. I never imagined when I came up with the screen name CEOBill that she'd turn a shortened "billionaire" into Billy. I remembered her calling my name when she came. Silas, not Billy. I wanted that again, not this nickname. But if this was the only way I could get her, especially since I was still in California, I'd take what I could get.

And I was getting her all to myself. Every sexy, fun minute. These calls were the highlight of my day. I enjoyed seeing her, the real her that peeked through.

Over the past few days, things slowly shifted. She appeared on the screen, and I got instantly hard seeing her all prim with her pearls, barely hiding her perky, lush tits. Okay, that hadn't changed at all. What had was that I took over. Every night we started with her taking off her panties, for a fee. Then she held them up for me, for another payment. It was worth it because I knew her pussy was bare while we talked. Then I led the conversation, even though I had to type. Then I got her to read book scenes that made her hot and I got to watch her squirm.

Your pussy ache, kitten? I asked tonight when she paused.

She put her ereader down and nodded at the screen. "I... I like that he took what he wanted."

You want it rough? A kitten like you?

Oh, she loved it rough.

Her eyes went hazy, and I had to wonder if she was thinking of the time I bent her over that desk and took her without much restraint. Or when she asked me to fuck her harder on the conference table.

"I think I might. I bet your dick is big and would cram me full, just like in the story."

It is. And I sure as fuck would.

I was stroking it now, although I had to stop and type often enough it drew the whole thing out. I was having insane orgasms with my hand. Alone in a hotel room just *watching* and *listening* to Eve. When I got her beneath me again, I was probably going to nut all over her before I got inside.

But I'm not there and your pussy's needy. Come for me.

She blinked. "Come?"

Touch yourself.

"Now? I um... don't do that on screen."

You do because you know I'm watching. You like it when you're watched. But you're safe because it's me.

This was pushing it, but I could tell she was horny. She couldn't fake the flushed cheeks. The hard nipples poking through her bra and sweater. The way she squirmed as she read.

She was as desperate as I was.

I'll watch you come.

"Remember, I don't do naughty things without incentive."

Money. Eve wanted me to pay her more. I did that for free on the conference room table. I pushed the donate heart icon and paid.

"Oh, this is going to be so naughty, isn't it? You watching while I make myself come?"

You're a dirty girl.

I imagined her on my bed, naked, legs parted and touching herself as I watched.

"Will you come with me?" she asked.

Yes.

Hell yes. I stroked myself as I watched her settle in.

She flopped back on the bed so she was angled and I could watch as she worked her dress up and a glimpse of a bare thigh. Her pussy was blocked because her leg was bent, but I could see her torso, her tits in that tight sweater, and the way her hand went down between her legs.

I couldn't see anything, but I saw *everything*. I watched her face and upper body as she fingered her hot little pussy and made herself come. Listened to her moan and arch her back.

I spurted all over myself remembering how she'd looked when she'd come on my dick.

Thick ropes of cum covered my hand and lower belly as she moaned and thrashed.

That's my good kitten. I love watching you play with that naughty pussy.

I had to get back to Hunter Valley. To Eve, to get her to do exactly this in person. Theo was right. I was going to get carpal tunnel with all the jerking off I was doing.

EVE

I STILL HADN'T HEARD from the big bank about my loan.

It was life as usual. Or mostly. I was up at five and ran the shop. Then at night I talked with Billy–the secret side of Silas.

"Tonight's reading is a CEO showing the college intern who's boss," I said as I laid on my back and worked my panties down my legs–after he paid me extra. Yes, my excerpt choice had been very intentional.

I was insane. Silas wasn't a stranger, but we weren't *together* either. All of the time we talked was in a cam room. Was this fucked up? Yes. Was knowing that Silas knew I cammed and keeping himself a secret while I pretended not to know it was him fucked up? Completely.

When he'd donated extra money and the panties were off, I held them up for him to see and read his response.

Do you want to be shown who's boss?

I bit my lip, thought about it. Nodded. Yes, I wanted to be dominated by Silas. Taken hard. I'd love it.

Undo the buttons and show me what's mine.

I pointed to the corner of the screen, and he donated more money.

This time, I didn't leave my cardigan closed by a few strong buttons. I undid all of them. My breasts in the black bra were revealed. For him.

That's a very naughty bra color. Panties too.

"I told you about me," I said. "What about you?"

I wanted to get him to talk. To reveal himself. To tell me he was really Silas and show his face.

What about me?

I thought for a moment, wondered how to push him. "What do you do?"

I run a company.

"Oh, CEOBill. Right. Is that why you won't show your face?"

Yes.

"If you have to keep it a secret, why are you on here?

You're successful and I'm sure handsome and... well, how come you're not taken?"

I have my eye on one woman.

Anger flared in me, and I did up the buttons on my sweater. "Oh?" I asked. No way in hell was I showing him my breasts and my wet panties if he was off fucking some other woman.

Shit. Maybe he was. I had no claim on him. Sure, he said he wanted me to ride him when he returned to Hunter Valley, but that didn't mean exclusivity.

Your jealousy makes me fucking hard.

"I'm not jealous," I snapped. I was jealous. So very jealous. And hurt.

The woman I have my eye on is you. You, kitten.

I felt bashful and thrilled. And angry.

He knew it was me and he did that? The jerk.

Inwardly, I smiled. Like June said, payback was a bitch.

"Well, that's nice to hear," I began, "but you're not the only man in my life."

Excuse me?

I shrugged, played coy and looked down at the quilt on my bed. "I'm tired of being a virgin. I mean, with you on here and all, all I've gotten is horny. Really, really horny. I have needs and well, I've found someone who can take care of them."

You met a guy and you're going to let him fuck you?

I nodded. "I've learned so much from being in here with you. From the sex scenes I'm reading aloud."

When?

"When am I going to sleep with him?" I grinned, played with my pearls. "Oh Billy, you know we're not going to sleep. I'm so wet all the time that I don't think one time's going to be enough to make this ache go away. And I'll let you in on a secret... his dick is really big."

God, I sounded like a real cam girl.

When?

I shrugged, then bit my lip. "Soon."

SILAS

I SLAMMED the lid on my laptop and snagged my cell. "Bradley, I want the plane ready in an hour."

"Where to?"

"Hunter Valley."

EVE

"MOTHER. What are you doing here this late?" I asked after I opened my front door.

I wasn't expecting her. Well, I never expected her because she'd never come to my house before. I was just glad I was done with my call with Billy... Silas, and I'd changed into sweats before she arrived.

She lifted a garment bag. "Dinner at the club with the Morgans went long. You know how they like to talk. I brought your dress and shoes."

"For what?" I asked, stepping back to let her in.

It wasn't snowing, but it was cold. I shut the door quickly behind her.

She stopped a few feet inside and stared. "This place is... quaint."

That meant she hated it. Not that I cared. It was a little mining cottage, built in the first years of the town. It had been updated–like a bathroom instead of an outhouse–and I found it perfect. It was just me and I didn't need much, especially on my rental budget. I never cared for the massive mansion I grew up in. I was an only child and so the nine bedrooms were a little excessive. But we were the Hunters and needed to have the best of everything. Including views. Kitchens. And large quantity of bedrooms.

"What's the dress for?" I asked, breaking her from frowning at my living room/dining room combination.

"The holiday party, of course. I told you about it on the phone." She held it out and I had no choice but to take it. She tugged off a leather glove, then the other. Her coat was black, long and cashmere. Her boots were suede, a surprise for this wet weather. Her hair was the same shade as mine, but while mine was in a sloppy bun, hers was styled to appear wind-blown, as if she'd been out zipping around on a snowmobile and came inside looking perfect.

"Right." She was expecting me to look at it, so I unzipped the bag and laid it over the back of my couch.

It was emerald velvet and from what I could tell it had a deep V.

"It's very pretty. Thank you."

"Cheney will wear a matching tie, of course."

"I'm not going with Cheney," I said immediately.

"Cheney is expecting you."

I crossed my arms, frowned. "That's his problem, not mine."

"Evelyn, it's the annual Hunter family holiday party. You can't go without a date."

I had to wonder if she was going deaf, if she needed ear candling or if she was playing dumb. Maybe she was actually insane because she expected me to fall in line with Cheney as my date. That he was in charge of my inheritance.

Nothing I said about Cheney was going to change her thoughts. To her, I was going to the party with him. I was going to marry him and have his babies and we were going to lounge about and lavishly spend money. My money.

It made no sense. Cheney was just a guy. His family was wealthy with their mine. The one that stripped the mountainside and was most likely an ecological disaster.

I went to the front door and opened it. Even someone as obtuse as my mother got the message, I wanted her to leave. "If you like Cheney so much, Mother, you take him."

30

SILAS

"You're back." Mav slapped me on the shoulder, then pulled me in for a brotherly hug. "Good to see you."

"Thanks."

The James Inn looked like a mountain lodge, with the thick log walls and river rock chimneys. Oversized windows offered views of the entire valley from every angle. There were ten suites in the main building, plus a few small cabins for those wanting more privacy. With an event space for weddings and other celebrations, the place would be busy. Like the other inns Mav had built from scratch, I was sure this location would be a hit.

The soft opening was in a few weeks. In the meantime, all the furniture was in. All that remained was staff training and stocking last minute items that were lost in shipping. It looked good and as CEO, I should care.

Right now, I didn't give a shit. Eve was going to fuck some stranger?

No fucking way.

"I didn't know we were meeting today," he said, his brain working through his calendar.

"We're not. I'm here for Eve," I said, looking around as I brushed snow off my shoulders. I was impatient. Frustrated. Horny.

Where the fuck was she? No way in hell was she sleeping with some asshole. Yeah, the virginity thing was just a cam room ploy to get a guy's dick hard–and it fucking worked–but she wasn't sleeping, or *not* sleeping, with anyone but me.

I needed to touch her. Lick her. Fuck her good and hard and hear *my* name coming from her lips so she'd forget whoever the asshole was who'd started sniffing around.

His eyes widened and a slow smile spread across his face. "Oh. Don't you have Hyport meetings?"

"Yes, but Bradley's taking them for me. I sent the CEO an email."

I had, late last night while on the flight to Hunter Valley. I wrote Robert personally, telling him that my bride needed me for a day and that my assistant would fill in. After our little chat in his office, I figured he'd understand.

"The woman at the coffee shop told me she was here."

When I flew out last night, I'd been thinking with my dick, which wasn't all that smart at logistics.

I landed after midnight and while I could have texted Eve to find out where the hell she lived so I could show up and fuck the hell out of her, she wouldn't be awake. Not a coffee shop owner whose doors opened at six. When I woke up this morning, I went directly to the shop, but fuck... she wasn't there.

"Yeah." He nodded. "She's stocking the cafe, the storeroom for the restaurant itself, and the coffee stations in each room."

I sighed. Fucking finally.

"That's a big contract for her," I said, impressed.

"Only the best for James Corp. We just finished and I sent everyone else home for the day since the weather is turning to shit. We're supposed to get a foot before dinner and then another two feet overnight. I hope you weren't planning on flying out later."

"I was."

"You aren't now. I was waiting for Eve to follow her back to town, but if you're here, I'll head out."

It was time to stake my claim. I'd been kidding myself that I was content fucking her on hard surfaces and then flying off to make business deals. Or just watching and talking with her in the cam room.

She needed to know I was the one who was fucking her from now on. Me and only me. Plus, I was tired of jerking off to a livestream of her on my laptop.

"I'll keep her safe," I replied, assuring him so maybe he'd fucking leave already.

"Good." He pointed behind me. "She's that way."

I headed toward the cafe where there was a small service counter and bakery case, both currently bare. There, facing the wall of shelves, was my woman. Fucking finally. I'd recognize that ass anywhere. She had on a thick fuzzy purple sweater, jeans, and shearling boots. Completely covered because it was fucking cold and snowing... and she wasn't on her bed in the cam room with me.

"Eve."

She spun around, a glass jar filled with coffee beans in her hand. Her face lit up. "Silas. What are you–"

I didn't give her time to talk further. I'd been across the country staring at her in sexy sweaters reading about being railed by a CEO through my laptop. She was in front of me.

I could touch her.

And kiss her.

So I did.

My naughty, sexy woman whose scent was citrus and coffee and somehow tasted like sweet pastry and sin. Her mouth and her pussy.

31

EVE

SILAS WAS KISSING ME. *Kissing* me. Not a peck, but an onslaught. A mouth assault. A... wow. One second, I was sprucing up the cafe with decorative jars of coffee beans, the next I was being kissed.

Oh.

Oh.

Silas turned so I bumped into the counter, then the wall, then the closed door, our teeth clashing.

"Shit, are you okay?" he asked, lifting his head so his eyes could search my face for harm.

"Yes, don't stop."

I had no idea how long we made out like

teenagers–*very* horny, aggressive teenagers–but Silas eventually pulled back.

His hand was cupping my breast beneath my sweater. His knee was wedged between my legs, and I was hoisted up riding his thigh. I was halfway to orgasm already.

"I was gone for too fucking long. I've wanted to do that... and more, since the conference room."

His voice was deep, ragged. Blue eyes sparkled with need and eagerness. Reaching up, I cupped his jaw, felt the softness of his short beard. I loved the scent of him. The hard feel of his body. The thick press of his erection against my hip. Of his entire body into mine.

He felt... powerful. Dominant. Bold.

"Silas. What are you doing here?"

"I couldn't wait any longer. I told you I wanted you to ride me. You said you were game. I've been imagining it since I left. You still want to climb in my lap and fuck yourself on my dick?"

I wondered if he was here because of the night before. My taunting. I wanted Silas. God, did I. But I wanted all of him. He couldn't keep Billy a secret and fuck me now.

"You left your meetings for me?" Bridget had told me about the hotel purchase he was negotiating. It had made it into some of the larger papers. A billion-dollar hotel chain didn't plan to buy out another without it making the news. And Silas was at the helm for all of it.

Leaning in, Silas kissed my neck, working his way up to the sensitive spot behind my ear. "Fuck yes, ki–" he murmured, then sucked on my skin as if he couldn't resist a second longer. His thigh shifted to rub over my clit. Fuck, that felt good.

What was it about Silas that made me lose my mind? What was it about the two of us and public places?

He almost called me kitten.

I pulled back. He was breathing hard, his gaze laser focused on my mouth and his hands kneaded my breasts and tugged my nipples.

"Why, Silas? Why now?" I asked, pushing him.

"Because I won't have you fucking anyone but me," he practically snarled. "No one else. And no more camming, kitten." His fingers pinched my sensitive tips. Fuck! "This body is all mine."

I had driven him here. My feminine wiles had worked. Maybe if he wasn't so... intent, he'd realize I wasn't freaking out.

I set my hands on his cheeks, rested my forehead against his.

"Oh Billy, it's always been yours."

32

SILAS

I WAS LOST in the feel of her skin against my lips, the soft swells of her tits and the way her nipples hardened beneath my palms. The way she arched her back and seemed to love a little rough handling. Then her words caught up to me.

Billy.

She'd called me Billy.

I froze, then stepped back.

"You. What? How? Oh. Kitten." I wiped my hand over my mouth, too aroused to process quickly. I'd called her kitten. The only time I called her that was in the cam room. Where she wasn't supposed to know I was Billy.

She nodded.

But she did.

"You knew?"

My dick was trying to break out of my jeans and get to Eve, but he'd have to wait.

Eve had known it was me in the cam room.

What the fuck?

"Yes. Not at first. I ended the one call early. I couldn't do it, the camming, with a stranger. It was... creepy. Then Bridget told me it was you who bought out my time."

"What?" I ran a hand through my hair, paced. Thought back. "So you've been in there with me, knowing it was me. Taunting me?"

A slow grin spread across her face. Her hair was messed up from my hands, her lips glistening and swollen. A flush spread across her cheeks and those nipples I just plucked were hard and eager for more.

"Yes," she replied, completely unrepentant. In fact, she looked amused. "You deserved it. You were taunting me in return."

I remembered how she'd messed with me the night before. "Who's the guy?"

"There's no guy," she said, rolling her eyes. "You made me jealous first, remember? I didn't like it."

"Yeah? I didn't like it either," I grumbled.

"Wait, are you mad?" She set her hand on my chest. "I'm the one who should be mad. Why didn't you tell me it was you?"

"Because you wouldn't take the money." I looked at her, processed more about the calls. Narrowed my gaze at her cunning. "You were milking me for extra money. With taking off the panties and all that."

She shrugged, clearly not bothered. "I told you I couldn't take your money with the loan and yet you went and did this instead."

"You thought camming and taking money from hundreds of horny strangers was better than not taking it from me? And it wasn't from *me,* it was James Corp."

"You're the one who flew across the country jealous, wanting me to ride your dick. You're the only one I won't take money from!"

I shook my head. "Kitten, you were being stubborn. Don't you know I only have you and your business's best intentions in mind?"

"Stubborn? You think my business decisions are made on a whim because I'm stubborn? Again, you're the one who flew here, interrupting your billion-dollar deal."

I rubbed my lower lip with my thumb, eyed her. Oh, she was formidable, and I wanted to fuck her harder for it.

"Now you have quite a bit of money to cover what you need for the coffee shop. Quite industrious of you."

She shook her head. "I'm not taking that money."

"What?" She'd be the first person *ever* not to want anything financially related from me.

"I'm donating all of it. I'm not using a dime, Silas James."

I shrugged. I didn't give a shit about the money. I only cared about her. By extension, that meant her coffee shop. If it was her dream, then I wouldn't see it fail. If not this way, then another. "Fine, donate it. Then we're back to where we were five seconds after I pulled out of you at the bar."

"Where's that?"

"With me horny as fuck and needing inside you. I know you're turned on too. Probably just as desperate for my dick."

Enough was enough. We could talk this whole fucking thing in circles for hours. That wouldn't solve my hard dick problem or the fact that I wanted to watch Eve scream my name.

Mine, not Billy.

I stepped close, tossed her over my shoulder.

"Silas!" she cried. "How do you know I'm desperate?"

I gave her ass a little swat as I went. "I paid a fortune for you to show me how soaked I made your little panties."

33

SILAS

I WENT up the massive staircase and entered the first room on the right. I spun around, faced Eve and got to work on her sweater, yanking it off her with an aggression and need I seemed to only feel with her.

She caught on, that I wanted us naked and toed off her boots. Clothes flung every which way and we laughed when my pants caught, inside-out, on my shoe and wouldn't come off.

Finally, FINALLY, she was bare. I was bare.

For the first time, I saw every inch of her gorgeous body. I took a moment to circle her.

Then I took her hand, walked backwards until the back of my legs hit the bed. I sat, then pulled her close.

Kissed her. Delved deep. Swallowed her moans. Her whimpers.

She lifted her head, smiled at me in a way that told me I might be in trouble. That she had plans.

"No more money. No more secrets," she said.

"Only my dick in your pussy," I added.

"Exactly."

With the slightest push on my chest, I fell back. If she wanted to be in charge, I was fine with that.

I laid on the bed, knees bent and my feet touching the floor, my dick pointing straight up.

Setting her hands on my thighs, she leaned forward and licked me like an ice cream cone.

My hips bucked involuntarily, surprising her. She pulled back and grinned.

"Get up here and sit on my face, kitten," I growled. I loved calling her that and could finally do it.

She was naked and I wasn't touching her. Her skin was pale, smooth. Soft. Lush. Curvy. Perfection.

"But I want you in my mouth," she said with a pout. "I want to feel how hard you are on my tongue."

Fuck me. I wasn't going to last two seconds if she did that. Still... if she wanted to suck me off, I wasn't going to stop her. I crooked my finger. "You can sit on my face while you suck my dick. You remember we talked about it. That first night."

Her eyes flared with surprise, then heat.

She did as I said and crawled up onto the bed, settled so she straddled my chest, then flipped around.

Fuck me, her pussy was gorgeous. Wet, pink. With lips and folds to suck and lick.

Taking hold of her hips, I pulled her back and onto my face.

"Silas!" she cried as my tongue slid over her from top to bottom and then back again.

Then stopped.

"Silas!" she said again, this time whipping her head around and glaring. "Why did you stop?"

"My dick's right there, kitten. Suck it."

As CEO, I gave the orders. People–everyone–did what I said. Stubborn Eve often didn't, but this time? Thank fuck, she was a very good listener. She turned back, licked the pre-cum that was beading at the top. Then my mind went blank when she took me into her mouth, and I got back to work eating out my woman.

34

EVE

EVEN THOUGH I read a scene with it from a romance book, I'd never done sixty-nine before. It was actually really hard. Silas was using his talented mouth and tongue on my pussy, and I couldn't focus enough to suck him very well. I had him in my mouth, working him, but then I'd find I stopped, doing nothing but moaning on his dick because I was so close to coming.

Then I remembered my task and went back at it. It seemed the better I did, the more voracious Silas became. It was a game called Distraction. Who could get the other out of their head and make come first?

Who won this one?

Silas.

Well, maybe me.

I had to lift off his dick as I cried out his name when I came. He manhandled me around so I was facing him, straddling his waist. Then he was lowering me down and onto him.

Setting my hands on his shoulders, I shimmied a bit as he filled me. Silas was big.

"Fuck, yes," he growled, then, "Shit."

I was lifted up and off.

"Silas–"

"You sucked me so good I forgot a condom," he said, his breath ragged as he reached for his pants on the floor. It was impossible since I was on top of him, and his pants were on the floor.

"I'm on the pill."

He stilled, stared at me, then flopped onto his back.

Hands stroked up and down my thighs, his hard, glistening dick between us. Bare.

His pale eyes met mine. "What are you saying, kitten? You're good going without a condom?"

I nodded. "I'm clean because after Cheney, well–" I stopped talking because who mentioned their ex when she was about to cowgirl up on a different guy's dick?

"I'm clean. I know it sounds crazy, but I've never gone without a condom. Not once. Trust me to take care of you."

I bit my lip, felt his words as much as heard them. Trust him. He wanted to take care of me.

I lifted up, gripped the base of him and lined him up again at my entrance.

He watched, entranced as I started to lower down again.

"This is all I've been thinking about," he admitted, his jaw clenched, his fingers digging into my hips. "Seeing you like this. Watching my dick slide into you. Fuck, you're so perfect. Fuck!" His head fell back and he practically growled.

It felt so good, so tight. I wasn't exactly sure how he fit, but he did. "It's like we're made for each other," I whispered. This was all I'd been thinking about, too. Sitting on his lap and riding him. Just as he'd texted.

"Eve."

Silas jackknifed up, wrapped his arms around me and kissed me. His beard was soft against my skin as our tongues met.

Then he helped me lift and lower, fuck myself on him until we came and were nothing but a perfect, sweaty, sticky mess.

35

SILAS

I STOOD in front of the machine in the cafe, waiting for my coffee to brew. I didn't really need it because I was wide awake at five a.m. The sun hadn't come up yet and Eve was out cold in our room. That was what five orgasms–or was it six?–did to her. I felt a shit ton of male satisfaction that I could please her so well. Fucking her into unconsciousness was now my new goal in life.

I'd picked up on the theme of the stories she read to me during the cam calls. A trend in her sexual interests. In what made her hot. She definitely liked being watched. Taken. Dominated.

I intended to fulfill every one of them.

But I still had to work and that meant starting the day with a daily update from Bradley.

"I told Hyport last night about the blizzard and that you're most likely snowed in for a day or two. I think he finds it romantic," he told me through the phone.

Mav's weather report had been accurate. A shit ton of snow had fallen, and it was still coming down. That meant I wasn't returning to San Francisco, and he'd have to continue to cover.

"I'm sure he watches that movie channel with all those holiday movies, being snowed in at a resort with a beautiful woman," I replied.

"You just described yourself."

I couldn't help but laugh. "Right. Except in the movie the assistant doesn't call at five in the morning."

"Romance movie or not, he'll want you back here. When do you think the roads will be cleared for you to get out?"

"Not sure." Didn't care.

I wasn't in a rush to work or do anything but take two coffees back upstairs and wake my woman the best way I knew how.

With my mouth on her pussy again.

Yeah, there was no decision. In bed with Eve or Hyport negotiations?

"Your agenda for today–"

"I'll pull it up to review," I said, cutting him off. "Who's up first this morning? Berlin or New York?"

"Neither. Your schedule is clear."

I didn't understand. "Clear?" I took a sip of the black coffee. Fuck, it was good.

"Yes. I rescheduled everything and I'll handle Hyport. Enjoy the coffee. And Eve."

How he knew I was making coffee, I had no idea.

36

EVE

"Mmm, that smells good," I murmured, rubbing my face into the soft pillow. The linens and bedding were exceptional. It felt like I was sleeping on a cloud.

The room was dark, only the moonlight coming through the window lit the room. We'd had our minds on other things the night before and hadn't closed it. With the snow, everything practically glowed.

Including Silas, who was naked. Just like all the mornings I'd watched him from my window.

I could see every ridge, every throbbing vein that ran up the long length.

I was used to waking early, but this? To have him

right in front of me when I opened my eyes? Amazing. I couldn't help but smile.

Not only did we have sex the night before... all night, but I got to sleep in his arms. Then wake up to him, his hard dick and coffee. What could be better than that?

"Do you always walk around naked?" I wondered.

"Mmm, in the mornings. Yes. I had plans on how I was going to wake you." He set two white mugs imprinted with the James Inn logo on the side table.

"Coffee's a good way to do that," I offered. "I love coffee."

"I had something better in mind than coffee. Besides, this might taste horrible. I don't run a coffee shop."

I smiled even broader and rolled onto my back, the blankets tucked beneath my arms. "You run hotels. This one, in fact. This bed is spectacular. Five stars. Would definitely recommend."

He grinned. "Good to know. You want coffee or my mouth on your pussy?"

God, I loved those choices. Suddenly, the bed was quite warm. I watched as his dick got hard, thickening and lengthening, then rising to bob up toward his navel. Up close, he was... perfection.

"Well?" he asked.

I lifted my gaze and he was smiling and offered me a wink. I was caught.

"Show me the mole on your butt. The one you told me about in the cam room."

He arched a brow, but turned, showed me his perfect ass. And the little mole. He glanced at me over his shoulder, then turned back.

"What'll it be, kitten? Coffee or my mouth on your pussy?"

I grinned, then pushed myself up so I leaned against the plush pile of pillows and the padded headboard. Then I shoved the thick down comforter down, kicked it to the foot of the bed. Reaching for the mug, I held it in front of my mouth and blew on the hot brew.

Bending my knees to give him room between them, I said, "Both."

He slowly crawled onto the bed with me. "You want me to eat you out while you have your first cup of coffee?"

"Multitasking at its finest."

Settling onto his stomach and placing his palms on my inner thighs to open me wider, he looked up my bare body. God, that was the perfect sight.

"Multitasking? This is my greatest skill."

"Prove it," I replied, right before he licked me and did just that.

37

SILAS

"When's the snowplow coming?" I asked Mav. I called him to find out when Eve and I had to stop fucking all over the inn and expect workers. From the second-floor window, I studied the drive that led to the county road. Or at least *where* the drive should be since it was buried in snow. The blizzard pushed east and now the sun was out, sparkles glistening on the pristine white surface. It was hard to look at it was so bright.

"You're right downtown," he replied. "I'd give it a few hours and you should get at least one pass by a plow," he replied.

"I'm not at the house," I told him. "I'm at the inn."

"You're at the inn?"

It was after lunch and Eve and I finally got dressed. Barely. After we had our coffee and I had her pussy, she reciprocated very skillfully. Then we fell back asleep. For hours. A late start was a treat for both of us. I agreed with Eve. The bedding was amazing.

So was the woman who shared it with me.

I'd slept with women in the past, but they'd been casual. I didn't remember sharing a bed with one longer than the fun it took to get off. No sleepovers. No napping.

Never one who'd fooled me in a cam room for several days and technically bilked me–or at least my dick–for thousands of dollars. That credit card bill was going to be insane.

"Yes," I said. "We never left."

Mav grunted.

Eve came up to me carrying a plate with a sandwich she made from the fixings in the restaurant fridge. She'd sliced it on a diagonal and loaded some corn chips beside it. I shook my head, turning down her offering as I held my cell to my ear. With a shrug, she took a bite herself.

"What do you mean *we?*" he asked.

"I'm here with Eve." With her name mentioned, she looked my way. I mouthed *Mav* and gave her a wink.

"You're there with Eve?" he parroted.

"Yes."

I heard him cover the phone and talk to someone,

probably Bridget, although I could hear it all clearly. "Yes, with Eve. At the inn. Yes. I know. Of course they're stuck there without the plows," he said as if Bridget was being obtuse, which was impossible.

"There's at least two feet. Maybe three," I told him. His house wasn't five miles away, but higher up in the hills. They could have more than here at the inn. "I've got an SUV, but the snow's too deep for it."

"I'll call the service that does my driveway and–"

"No plowing! No plowing!" Bridget called.

"–they could be there sometime this afternoon. No way workers will show up, so you have the place to yourselves."

"Yes, leave them there," Bridge said, her voice carrying.

"Why should we leave them there?" Mav asked her.

"He needs to tell her the truth about the camming!"

Eve nabbed a corn chip, oblivious to the conversation in my ear. I took her in. The same clothes as the day before, but I knew she wasn't wearing anything beneath. No bra. No panties. Her hair was a tousled mess, and she must've found a hair tie in her purse because it was up in a sloppy bun.

No makeup, well rested, well satisfied, she was fucking gorgeous.

I crooked a finger and she came over. I kissed the top

of her head and wrapped an arm around her so her back was to my front. She felt soft. Warm.

Mine.

And mine alone.

No workers. No access to our jobs or the outside world.

I had Eve all to myself and just like Bridget had suggested, no plowing. *Leave them there.*

"Don't worry about it," I told Mav.

"What?" Mav asked, surprised. "You–oh. Ow! Baby, that fucking hurt. You want a spanking, don't you?"

"No plowing at the inn!"

I imagined Bridget smacking Mav and tried not to laugh. He was a tank and she was tiny. "Fine, we're leaving you," he replied. "Tomorrow then?"

I thought about it. Tomorrow? Would that be enough time to have Eve all to myself?

Hell no.

"The next day. And tell Bridget that Eve knows."

He did and I heard Bridget in the background. Was she clapping?

He laughed. Finally, he caught on. "Got it. Not tomorrow. Have fun."

"We will," I said, then hung up, snagging a corn chip, then taking the plate from her and setting it on the arm of the reading chair tucked into the cozy bay window.

"Hey! We're sharing that!"

I spun her to face me, leaned down and tossed her over my shoulder. Now that I knew we would be alone for a while, I was going to take full advantage.

"Are you always going to do this? Carry me around like a sack of potatoes?"

"Oh, kitten, you have no idea."

She laughed.

"Did they have whipped cream in that fridge?" I asked, heading for the kitchen. Licking food off her body became very important.

She stopped squirming. "Maybe. Definitely chocolate syrup."

My dick went from a semi to full-on hammer. "Even better."

Fuck, this was so much better than work.

38

EVE

"WE WENT over this in the cam room. Pink's my favorite color. What's yours?" I asked.

We were sprawled across a couch in the lobby. Silas lay sideways on it and I was on top of him. His hand was resting on my ass. Oh, and we were naked. Again. He'd started a fire in the massive fireplace. Thankfully, the nook for wood had already been filled. The storm had stopped a few hours earlier and outdoors was a post-blizzard winter wonderland. We had heat, electricity, fire, and food. And chocolate syrup. We were content.

And sated. I lost track of how many orgasms he gave me. How many places we fucked.

There was the bed.

The prep counter in the kitchen.

The wall in the dining room.

The registration desk.

This sofa, which probably, along with every other spot, needed to be well sanitized before the opening.

I hadn't thought about anything at all outside of the little bubble we were in. Or was it a snow globe?

No plows meant no escape. I worried about the shop remaining closed, but Silas had said no one would head out to get coffee. If they did, they'd understand why the shop wasn't open. I let it go.

I let everything go except being with Silas.

We were taking a break before we christened some other spot in the inn, just talking.

I was... happy. Being snowed in with him, I knew I was all in. This guy, he was amazing. Perfect. Ridiculously bossy. Hot. Sexy. Silly, even.

"Just like your pussy. Nipples, too," he murmured, his hand on my butt sliding inwards so the fingertips brushed my center. "Mmm, like that?"

I smiled and kissed his chest. "You know I do, but you're distracting me on purpose."

"Why would I do that?" he asked.

"Because you don't want to tell me what your favorite color is."

I felt his laugh, the slight shaking of his body beneath mine. "Tan."

I lifted my chin and looked in his eyes. "Your favorite color is *tan*?"

He shrugged and it moved us ever so slightly. "I don't know. I never really thought of it. I never really bought my own clothes."

"Your favorite color isn't only tied to clothes. It could be what you paint the walls in your house."

"My apartment walls are tan. Are yours pink? Fuck, will I come over and lose my mind knowing your place is painted the same shade as those plump little nipples?"

I squirmed because this was foreplay. Ridiculous, but it was working. "No."

"Well, I'm more in tune with my favorite color than you are then. Walls, clothes. Obviously, when I was a kid the personal shopper dressed me and my brothers, so tan had to be her favorite, too."

"Obviously," I countered.

"When I got old enough to shop for myself, I hired my own personal shopper because I had no clue what I was doing. Now my clothes magically appear in my closet clean, pressed, and ready to wear."

"Wow, a clothing fairy."

I thought of how I'd watched him in the mornings, naked in his house.

Still foreplay.

"My mother chose my clothes growing up. A few things now, too. Those cardigans in the cam room were thanks to her." I thought of the velvet dress for the holiday party and the foreplay was over. "Except for the Steaming Hotties t-shirts. The torn jeans. Oh, and the dangly earrings I love so much. Those are definitely not her doing. The other night, she brought over a dress for me to wear to their annual holiday party. It's a Hunter thing." It usually explained everything and I didn't have to say more.

"As in the Hunters of Hunter Valley."

"Right."

"If the dress she bought for you is a problem, know that I really like you naked," he said, giving my butt a firm squeeze.

"I like you naked, too." And up close. It was *so* much better up close.

SILAS

THEO TEXTED.

> Heard you're stuck at the inn with Eve.

My brothers were the biggest fucking gossips.

> Worried about me?

> No. And I'm no longer worried about your dick or your carpal tunnel.

Fucker.

SILAS

I LEANED AGAINST THE WALL, taking in Eve, in just my shirt, fixing us coffee. Decaf this time because we'd gone through a lot of fucking coffee. I'd mastered the simple coffee maker in the cafe area. Add water, add grounds to a filter, turn on. The fancy espresso machine was another story.

Watching her was the sexiest thing I've ever seen, and I seemed to be doing it a lot. Just watching her.

Eve could make coffee in a man's shirt and kill it camming. The virgin librarian version of her would have serious competition.

To me, her efficient and skilled actions were porn. Especially in my shirt.

But no more camming. This time, she was here, in front of me. Where she belonged. Where I could see her. Touch her. Make her mine.

"Take off the shirt," I said.

She spun on her bare feet, startled. The machine hissed behind her. Her eyes raked over me in my jeans. On, but not buttoned. Nothing else. "What?"

"Make me coffee. Bare."

She softened and responded to my deep command. Her lids lowered, cheeks flushed. And she started to squirm, just like she did in the cam room when she was turned on. "Silas."

I approached, cupped her face. "I want all of you," I admitted.

"You want more sex."

Her gaze dropped and the way my dick was tenting my jeans, it was pretty obvious.

"Always. But I like this. You and me."

Her dark eyes held something. Wariness. Hope. Many things. "This was just sex. A little fling at that bar."

"It *was* just sex. This isn't little, what's between us. I want more. Don't you?" I held my breath.

"We started out the wrong way," she admitted.

There was nothing wrong about us. "The quickie in the bar?"

"All of it. The quickie, the conference room. Especially the camming."

I set my hand on her shoulder, leaned in so we were eye level. "I'm CEO. I fix things. Help people. Giving you money does that. Why won't you keep the money from the cam room? It was as much my fault as yours."

"Because–"

Her cell rang and the moment was broken. She pulled back from my touch, went to see who it was. Picking it up from the counter beside the espresso machine, her shoulders slumped.

"Fuck," she whispered.

I went to her instantly. "What's the matter?"

It kept ringing.

"My father." She swiped the screen and answered. "Hello."

I could hear a male voice, but it was too soft to make out words.

I stepped back, grabbed one of the coffees that she made and leaned against the counter.

Her body language became tense. Her gaze was on her bare feet.

"Yes. Yes. No, I don't need money. No. I'm not interested in anything Cheney has to say. That's his problem. No. No, I wouldn't want to upset Mother. Yes."

She kept her eyes down as she ended the call and set the cell back on the counter.

I put my mug down, then wrapped my arms around her from behind. "Do I need to bury any bodies?"

A laugh shook her body. "No. Maybe."

"What happened?"

Instead, I wanted to take this sudden sadness from her. To make things right so she was happy. Always happy. Taking care of Eve was something I wanted to do. Not out of obligation, but a Neanderthal need to protect.

She was more than sex. She was my woman, and her problems were mine to take on and solve.

"My father wondered if I had any luck with getting other financing. He knew... KNEW... I couldn't get any other loan in town because he called the banks."

I spun her around. Her hands settled on my bare chest, and I looked down into her sad eyes. Not angry, but sad. Resigned. Destroyed.

"Your father told the banks not to give you a loan?"

"Yes." Tears welled, then slipped down her cheeks.

I tried to stay relaxed, to not let her feel how fucking pissed I was. The man was an asshole. I knew what a shitty father was like. Thought mine was the worst. He'd done nothing for me and my brothers except make us feel like shit about ourselves and our dreams. Shaming was an excellent tool.

She dropped her forehead to my chest, and I cupped the back of her neck, kissed her head. This wasn't the naughty little kitten on the cam. This was Eve, unvarnished. No makeup. No pretense. Truly bare. Her weaknesses and vulnerabilities exposed.

I ached for her. Ached to make her sorry shit-of-an-excuse father love her like she deserved. That wasn't going to happen, so I could help her in other ways. Hold her. Kiss her. Know that there was someone who wanted her just the way she was.

"Aren't fathers supposed to be supportive?" she asked.

"I wouldn't know. My father was a narcissistic prick."

"We should get them together," she replied.

"Mine's dead."

"Like I said, we should get them together."

I agreed with that. Killing the guy was probably out, but I was going to find out what he was up to. He was using his daughter for a reason, for his gain. I wanted to know what and why.

"Fathers can be assholes," I said.

"Yes. And this is why I won't take your money."

"Your father?"

"I care about you, Silas. I won't have money ruining us. Because it would. It ruins everything."

"Or maybe the people who are supposed to love you unconditionally are total dicks."

She laughed. "That is a possibility."

"Somehow, you need to let it go. Let him go. You can–"

"Are you mansplaining toxic parenting to me?"

I couldn't help but grin. "Maybe."

She smiled, but it quickly slipped away. "He made the local banks turn me away. What's next?"

That was a good question. I was the fixer, and I was going to fix this.

41

SILAS

SADLY, yet skillfully, the plow arrived and cleared the snow for us to get back to town. It also made a path for workers to get back to their projects at the inn. We had no choice but to leave. While the roads were cleared, they were snow packed, and I followed Eve to Steaming Hotties to make sure she got there safely. While I itched to keep her snowed in and trapped with me again, real life waited.

My cell rang as I pulled in front of my little house.

"Mr. Hyport. Hello," I said, shutting off my car.

"Silas. I understand you were snowed in."

I took in the piles and piles of snow. "That's right.

Haven't seen a storm like this one in a while. The plows are finally getting ahead of the three feet."

"Good. I'll see you back here for meetings tomorrow."

"Yes. Definitely."

"Oh, and Silas?"

"Yes."

"Bring your wife."

Wait. What? "Excuse me?"

"I want to meet her. The idea that this sale is keeping you two apart bothers Mrs. Hyport."

"She has a coffee shop to run," I said. This time, it was the complete truth. The only woman I had in mind as my wife was Eve. Although usually a woman knew when she was married.

Which we weren't. Because I lied to save the deal.

"We'll put you up in the Sausalito Suite. A second honeymoon. See you tomorrow."

Well fuck.

42

EVE

"You're leaving."

I knew when Silas came in that he was going somewhere. He wasn't in jeans, but dress pants. The kind no one in Hunter Valley wore, not now with feet of snow on the ground, piled high outside the shop's windows to make a small path on the sidewalk. It had only been a few hours, but he didn't have that same relaxed look that had settled about him while we'd been stuck at the inn. Of course, it could have been all the orgasms.

June took over the service counter and we stepped to the side. She knew we'd been stuck together, and I'd filled her in on some of what we'd done. Not the sexy stuff, but the fact that we'd both come clean about the cam room craziness.

It had only been three hours since he'd had his way with me this morning just as the sun was coming up. Me, bent over the side of the bed as he took me. Hard. Rough. Thoroughly as I'd gripped the sheets as if they might keep me anchored. I still felt him.

I was going to miss him. And his Big Dick. Stuck together with nothing to do but have sex, talk, and have more sex made me spoiled.

Reaching out, he tucked my hair behind my ear. A small gesture, but intimate. Familiar in a way that indicated we were... more.

He didn't have to answer. He trimmed his beard.

"Yes."

He suddenly looked uncomfortable, especially when he rubbed the back of his neck.

"I... um, need a favor. A really big favor."

"Okay."

He took a big breath. "I need you to be my wife."

I blinked. Was the Gregorian Chants coming from the speakers too loud? "I'm sorry, what? I think you just said you need me to be your wife."

He glanced at me, then away. "I did."

Not *want*. Need. He needed me to be his wife. No declarations of love. This wasn't a proposal.

"Why?"

What had happened in the past few hours?

He kept scrubbing his hand over the back of his neck.

Finally, he met my gaze. "The Hyport deal... during a meeting, they overheard you in the cam room. Reading a sex scene."

My cheeks heated and I covered my face with my hands. "Oh my God."

"Then I switched meeting times so I could be done at seven to join you in the room."

This was getting worse by the second.

"Robert, that's the CEO, pretty much cornered me and accused me of having a porn addiction."

I lowered my hands and looked at Silas. He looked frustrated and forlorn. A little scared and a little angry.

Silas, the epic organizer and master CEO, got caught watching porn. Not just porn. Me.

"I think I should've just taken that loan," I said.

His eyes widened in surprise and then started to laugh.

"None of this insanity would have happened if I did," I reminded him. "Although the animal shelter will probably disagree since they're thousands of dollars richer."

"I wouldn't have known all your sexy secrets though, kitten," Silas finally said when he could catch his breath.

I blushed because I had definitely, inadvertently, given away a lot.

"I'm still expecting you to maybe kill me with a coffee stirrer for telling you all this."

"Yeah, well, it's kind of hilarious. You, a porn addiction?"

He grinned, leaned close so his mouth brushed over my ear. "I'm a sex addict when it comes to you."

I shivered, knowing that was probably true.

"The deal could be blown because you're so sexy."

My smile slipped. "That's not funny, Silas."

He sobered up, too.

"Right. My father was going to merge with him twenty years ago, except my father slept with Hyport's assistant–on his desk apparently–and did some other shady shit. The deal fell apart. I've been trying to make it happen ever since I took over James Corp. It's almost done and then–"

I winced. "Then I happened."

He nodded. "Yeah. In the spur of the moment, I told him it wasn't porn, but my wife. My wife I hadn't told anyone about because I made her up right then and there. He doesn't seem to care if we do kinky shit in the confines of marriage."

"But not out," I clarified.

"Exactly."

He took my hands and held them between his. "I need you... desperately, to come to San Francisco and be my wife."

This wasn't how I expected a marriage proposal to go. Then again, I never expected to be a cam girl either.

"Evelyn," a deep voice called.

I stilled, then frowned. I didn't need to turn around to know that it was Cheney interrupting us.

I looked over my shoulder. "What?"

"If this is how you treat customers, then–"

I turned around to face him. Grumpy. "This is how I treat *you*. What do you want?"

He glanced around. "To see how the place is holding up."

"No snow damage. As you can see from the line, obviously business is good."

The tables were also full. Everyone in Hunter Valley had cabin fever. Except me. I wanted to go back to the James Inn and stay cozy all alone with Silas.

"Not for long," he said, his voice laced with acid.

Silas set his hand on my shoulder. I felt it. The hand. His presence. He had my back. "Right, because my father got all the banks in town to refuse me a loan."

He smiled. He fucking smiled. Which meant he knew. That didn't surprise me at all.

"Guess you have to come back to me after all."

I felt Silas's fingers tighten on my shoulder. I could feel the restraint, the barely-there reserve he held. Someone was fucking with me, and he didn't like it.

"Yeah, not happening," I said. "As I told you last time, I'm paying my bills just fine."

"How?" he asked, looking totally stumped. "No bank in town will give you money. Your trust is cut off. What are you doing to keep this place open?"

Wait. *Wait.*

I glanced at Silas over my shoulder. He needed me to marry him for his mega-deal to go through. Cheney wasn't going to let me do anything with my trust money. I had to wait until I turned thirty to access it. And to get him out of my life.

There was one way to solve my Cheney problem. Marriage, the other stipulation to my trust. If I got married–not to him–he wouldn't be in control of my money or me.

I wasn't sure if I would have thought of it if Silas hadn't suggested it first.

Everything would be resolved. Cheney would be gone. There would be no more reason to talk about the James Corp loan. Or the camming. Or covering any of Steaming Hotties' bills. Even my father and him getting the local banks to deny me a loan wouldn't matter.

I might be doing Silas a favor, but he could do one for me as well.

Maybe he didn't want me to be his wife, but he needed me. Well, I suddenly needed him in return.

"Cheney, did you meet my husband?" I asked.

43

EVE

I HOPED, crossed my fingers and toes, that Silas would play along. He was the one to suggest being married in the first place, but I doubted he expected to use it now. As in thirty seconds after he brought it up.

But I needed Silas to be my husband to get a hold of my trust fund. My money worries would be over. It was *my* money, so it was ridiculous that I had to go to such lengths to get it. I also doubted my grandparents had this in mind when they added the stipulation into their wills.

I also doubted they'd have an asshole like Cheney controlling the trust either.

If Silas needed my help, then I needed his. What did

it matter if it wasn't a real marriage? Love was always tied to money somehow.

This would be a mutually beneficial arrangement. And the sex was amazing.

"What the hell are you talking about?" Cheney's beady gaze shifted from me to Silas and back. "Husband?"

Reaching past me, Silas held out his hand for Cheney. "I'm Silas James. You are?"

"Cheney Douglas," he replied, more out of habit than the desire to make small talk.

"My ex," I explained.

They shook hands and kept shaking hands. Cheney's face was turning red, and Silas wasn't letting go. It was like a pissing contest, although it wasn't needed. I knew exactly which one had the bigger dick. And more talented.

"This guy?" Cheney asked. "He's paying your bills?"

Not only was he a jerk, he was a total misogynist.

"Paying her bills?" Silas made a scoffing sound. "Please, she married me for my dick."

I laughed, then swallowed it down based of the murderous look on Cheney's face.

"You're really married?" Cheney glanced at my hand. "I don't see a ring."

"I work in a coffee shop. Not the best place for the huge one he gave me."

With Silas beside me now, his arm still slung about my shoulders, I saw him shrug. "Five carats may not have been the best choice. Sorry, kitten," he added, kissing the top of my head.

Silas stopped his caresses on my shoulder, which was a shame, and looked to Cheney. "Your name is Douglas? Is it your family that owns that strip mine in the next county?"

"Yes," he replied, practically preening that Silas knew about their success.

"That's the one that's up for environmental review due to ecological impacts, right?"

Cheney's face turned a mottled red, no longer proud, but angry. "What the hell are you–"

"I wonder who the county commissioner is," Silas continued, cutting Cheney off. "I mean, if Eve's father can sway the local banks against his own daughter, then a guy like me might be able to sway some podunk, backwater politicians to shut your mine down."

My mouth fell open. How did he know all this? Did I care? Not really. The look on Cheney's face, a mixture of surprise and the possibility of a stroke was... awesome.

"You're back," June said, coming up and interrupting us and snarling at Cheney. "Here's another coffee for you. I made it just like last time. *To go.*"

She shoved the small carry-out cup into his hand,

and I imagined it to be laced with more powdered laxative.

"This isn't over," Cheney snapped. He gave his snooty glare to all three of us before grabbing the coffee and leaving. For being so rich, he didn't turn down something free.

Silas turned me, set his hands on my shoulders and looked me in the eye. "I'm staying to make sure that asshole doesn't come back."

June waved off his words. "He's not coming back today. Trust me," she said before heading back behind the counter. "Oh, and Eve, the sink's still dripping."

"Do I want to know how she's confident in that?" he asked. "About Douglas not coming back, not the sink."

I shook my head, tried not to smile. "Probably not. Just don't get on her bad side."

"What's up with the sink?"

I waved it off. "Nothing really. Just a little leak."

"Get me a list of anything that needs fixing."

"Not necessary. How did you know that stuff about Cheney and his family's mine?" I wondered, trying to stay on the important stuff.

"When Mav was looking for parcels of land to buy for the inn, the mine came up as a problem for us. Views, environmental impact, zoning, the whole deal. I read a report on it."

"Well, thanks for being there for me, husband," I replied. Was it okay that I pulled that out?

He leaned in close, met my eyes. "No one messes with you, Eve. Including an ex. Hell, especially one. He needs to know it's over."

"I've been telling him for almost a year."

He grunted, as if he didn't like that and had thoughts in his head about changing that.

"I want that fix-it list. I'm putting your ex on it. I'll make sure that was the last time he comes around."

"Oh," I said, feeling my cheeks heat. I liked having someone on my side for once. "Um... about that wedding. It needs to be the real deal." I couldn't get control of my trust otherwise. But more importantly, I added, "Cheney's going to look into the paperwork for it first thing."

Silas nodded. "I understand. Hyport probably will, too."

"My cousin Hunter's the sheriff and justice of the peace. We can get the license from him."

I couldn't believe we were talking about getting married at the same time we were bickering about shop maintenance.

"Good. I can't wait to make you mine."

Oh my.

44

SILAS

WE WERE MARRIED in the interrogation room of the Hunter Valley Police Station. Turned out, Eve's cousin Hunter, the sheriff, wasn't actually a justice of the peace. But the station manager was. For the ceremony, there were no flowers. No rings. No wedding dress; instead a pink Steaming Hotties t-shirt. Witnesses were two deputies who brought in a drunk and disorderly tourist from Omaha. If he were sober, he could have signed the documentation, too.

To me, it was perfect because it was Eve I was saying vows to. This was real.

When I asked her to be my wife, had I expected to *actually* marry her? No. I hoped, crossed my fingers, that she'd perhaps, maybe, hopefully agree to be a fake wife for a few days. It was asking a lot, I knew. Except she didn't want a fake marriage. She wanted the real thing.

Nothing went as expected with her.

My usual calm, orderly, over-traveled, and boring life had gone a little crazy.

For the good.

As we faced each other, I held her hands in mine, looked into her slightly-stunned gray eyes and vowed to honor, cherish, and protect her all the days of my life. I felt it to my very core.

We'd left directly from the police station and to the airport. Eve hadn't packed a bag. With the flight plan submitted and another storm ready to blow in, there had been no time before we had to leave. Now we were at forty-thousand feet, and I had her all to myself. Dot, the flight attendant, served us drinks before takeoff and had joined the pilots in the cockpit.

We were all–mostly–alone.

Reaching over, I unclipped her seatbelt, then pulled her into my lap.

"Silas!" she said with a laugh, pushing her hair back from her face.

"I'm going to fuck you before we get to San Francisco, but we need to talk about that asshole Douglas first. I'm not talking about other men when I'm inside *my* wife."

Her eyes flared with heat. She liked the idea of

joining the mile high club, but didn't seem too thrilled to talk about her ex. It wasn't like I wanted to either, but something was going on and I needed to know about it now so I could take care of the problem.

From what she said, he'd been sniffing around for a while and that wasn't working for me. Not with *my wife*. I was the only one who should be sniffing her.

Before we left the coffee shop, I'd sent a text to Bradley to find out all there was about Cheney Douglas. But I wanted to hear about him from Eve.

"Why did you introduce me to Douglas as your husband?" I wondered.

"I guess I need you as much as you need me," she admitted, and I realized she wasn't talking about sex or orgasms. No, she meant money. Fuck, I started all this by needing her to be my wife because of the Hyport deal–aka a billion dollars–but I knew I wanted her as mine.

It sounded like she never considered the possibility.

Not good. Another thing I needed to take care of. She needed to know that she was important. That she was special. That she was mine to care for. And fuck.

"I went to boarding school in Vermont," she began. Since she went so far back as to talk about high school, this wasn't a simple answer. "Senior year, when I came back for Christmas, I had dinner with my parents at the club with Cheney and his parents. It was announced over appetizers we were dating."

What the hell?

"You went along with it?" Obviously she did since the asshole lingered years later.

She shrugged. "I was seventeen. He was handsome. Older. At first he was charming. Plus, it was easier to go along with my parents than to make a fuss. I went back to Vermont and graduated, then went to college. I saw him on breaks."

"Did you even like him?"

She flushed and glanced away. "If you met my parents, you'd know there were expectations I was supposed to meet. I met them growing up because if I didn't, they did something like ship me to boarding school."

I clenched my jaw and stayed quiet. Remembered Bridget's story about the show chickens.

"After college, I broke up with Cheney. I was back in town full time and couldn't avoid him. I didn't *want* anything to do with him. I started Steaming Hotties using some money from a trust fund left to me by my grandparents."

She shifted and took off her sweater. Her long hair swung over her back as she dropped it on her empty seat. Yeah, it was getting warm on the plane.

I frowned, trying not to get distracted by the way her Steaming Hotties t-shirt stretched across her perfect tits. "Did you use it all?"

She shook her head.

"Then why did you apply for the James Corp loan?"

"Because I can't touch it until I'm thirty without permission of the executor. My father."

"He refused more money, I'm guessing."

She played with the frayed edges of the hole in the knee of her jeans. I liked the sexy peek at her bare skin.

"He told me I'd had my fun and it was time to close up my little shop and return home and marry Cheney."

I frowned. "Return home? I thought they lived in town."

With ease, she toed off one boot, then the other. They thumped on the carpeted floor.

"They do. Up by the resort. I was supposed to marry Cheney, head charitable functions, and push out a few kids."

I was all for a few kids, but it sounded like they wanted a Stepford Wife.

"I refused, obviously. I'd been broken up from Cheney for a while at that point and none of them accepted my decision. My father shifted the executorship to Cheney."

I was a businessman, not an estate lawyer, yet I knew this wasn't normal. "What? Why would he do that?"

It made no sense. Her father had her by the proverbial balls himself. Why relinquish that control besides just being a dick? What father put his daughter's ex-boyfriend in charge of her trust fund?

"Cheney told me I wasn't getting any more money from my trust and that I was to come back and marry him."

"So you married me instead. He can't be your husband if I already am."

Her fingers went to the hem of her t-shirt and slid it up her body, baring a delectable inch of her creamy skin at a time. I reached out and stilled her hands–like a moron–before she got it overhead, although her bra-covered breasts were exposed. I couldn't miss her hard nipples through the thin material.

"Um, what are you doing?"

She glanced my way, gave me that sly smile I remembered from the cam room. "You said we were going to fuck."

"Yeah, but not until after we talk about your ex."

"Okay, I'm just getting ready then."

My dick went from semi to rock hard in two seconds flat. I was practically dizzy from it and my fingers itched to touch her. My mouth salivated to taste her.

She didn't care that the flight attendant might make an appearance.

"Fuck, kitten."

"The answer to your question is yes."

Yes? "What was my question?" I asked, my gaze affixed on her tits.

When I let go of her arm, she flung off her t-shirt. It went somewhere behind me.

"If I married you so Cheney couldn't. Yes. That's one part of it, definitely."

All the blood had left my brain and was in my dick. I wasn't sure if I wanted to know the rest or could process what she was saying.

"The only other way I can take control of my trust–besides turning thirty–is to marry."

She stood, shimmied her jeans down her legs, then off.

Oh. Fuck.

"Wait," I said, gripping the arms of the seat. I had to stay focused, but it was nearly impossible with her only in her barely-there panties. If she turned around and I discovered it was a thong, I was going to come all over myself.

"What?" she asked. With her leaning forward, her tits practically spilled out of her bra.

I was practically panting now. "Douglas... Douglas won't be executor of your trust because you gain full control now that we're married. You get your money and get rid of the loser."

She nodded. "Yeah."

"Why didn't you ask me to marry you before now?"

Her eyes widened, then she laughed. "What would you have said to the woman who you fucked over a desk if she asked you to marry her?"

If she showed me all of her body like she was now, the answer would have been yes.

"Uh…"

"I know you've been with women before, but picture one of them."

I shook my head, studied the curve of her waist, the hint of her pussy lips through her panties. Was the satin damp? I knew they were fucking drenched.

FUCK.

"Other women, kitten?" I met her gorgeous gaze. "I can't see their faces or remember their names now."

"Because they meant so little to you."

"No, because I only see you. Fuck, Eve." I grabbed her, pulled her onto my lap again, this time so she straddled my hips. So her pussy settled right on my dick.

Her mouth dropped open. "Oh."

Yeah, she felt that, too. I rolled her hips as I lifted up mine.

She groaned. I growled.

"I get your point. I'd have thought you were crazy, or after my money."

"Exactly," she breathed, starting to rock all on her own.

"I think you've made it more than clear that you don't want any of my money."

She nodded, stared into my eyes. "It's just as you told Cheney. I want you for your big dick."

And that was it. I was done. My willpower was only so strong.

I ripped those panties off and yes, they were a thong, and had my dick out and deep in her in record time.

"Yes!" she cried as she took all of me in one go.

"Fuck, kitten," I growled as she rippled and clenched around me.

I had questions. A shit ton of them. But now wasn't the time.

I was fucking my wife. Nothing else mattered.

45

EVE

I WOKE to the scent of coffee. More luxurious sheets. And Silas naked.

I smiled as he handed me a mug, steam wafting from the top.

"Good morning," I said.

"Good morning, wife." He gave me that lazy smile of a well satisfied male. I'd made him that way and I felt immensely proud of myself.

His hair was damp and he smelled clean. Soapy.

I liked the sound of being called wife. Was it crazy? Yes. I was here in San Francisco to help him finalize his deal with Hyport. As his wife.

I blew on the top of my coffee, then took a sip.

"It's good, but not your coffee."

I agreed with him. It was good, but generic. I wasn't a coffee snob, but it was my thing. My job. It was important to me that my product was the best, even if it was for customers in a small town.

"I mix my own beans to get the blend just the way I like it," I admitted. "With a hotel this size, I'm sure they have a contract with a base distributor that collects beans from everywhere they can get a deal and make a generic mix from that."

He sat on the edge of the bed, studied me.

"That's not the way to do it?"

I took another sip. "It's one way. I source from a farm in Costa Rica I went to visit in college. If I were to work on a large scale like this..." I paused, glanced around the room as I thought. "I'd keep the distribution there, to support the local infrastructure and economy, but get a custom blend specifically for me."

"You know your stuff," he commented, then had a sip from his own mug. Frowned. "Yeah, not yours."

He moved about the room, pulled on a pair of boxers and I saw the little mole. I watched as I worked through my coffee. Was being his wife the right thing to do? Was marrying him so he could save his deal and so I could get my trust the right thing to do? Maybe not, but after last night? After what we did on the plane, then here in the bed, I felt like we had a solid basis for a marriage: amazing sex.

"We're expected for dinner with the Hyports at six. Since I'm behind from being snowed in with you, I'm in meetings all day."

I pushed myself up in bed and leaned against the headboard. "I don't have anything to wear." I held up my hand. "I don't mean that in a vacuous way, but Silas, I literally have no clothes."

His gaze roved down my body even though everything below my shoulders was beneath the plush comforter.

"I think I like you this way best."

"I can't meet the owners of the Hyport Hotel chain naked. That's kinda what got you into this mess in the first place."

He tugged on his pants. "This is San Francisco. Go out and buy some things." He went to his wallet that was on the bedside table, pulled out a credit card. A black one. "Here."

"What's this?" I asked, taking the very exclusive card. I recognized it because my father had one and gave it to my mother just like this often enough.

Slipping his arms into a crisp white dress shirt–how had it stayed so wrinkle-free in his bag?–and began to button it.

"My card. Buy what you want. Check out the spa downstairs."

Buy what I wanted. Spa? I felt like I was in the movie *Pretty Woman*. No, worse. I felt like my mother.

I could buy my own clothes. Pay for a massage. I was independent, not reliant on him, or I thought I was.

I was here as an accessory for Silas, physical proof that he wasn't a creepy manwhore like his father. I was to prove he was a decent guy for Mr. Hyport to sign on the dotted line. I'd show up for dinner, meet the Hyports. Look pretty. Smile.

He set a hand on the bed and leaned in. Kissed me. I'd been thinking so hard that I missed him button his shirt and put on a tie.

"I'll be back to get you at five-thirty. Meet in the lobby?"

I could only nod as he grabbed his suit jacket and left the bedroom. I heard the click of the suite's main door when it shut behind him.

This was another role. I needed the right outfit. I had no doubt a cardigan and pearls would work for this as well, although with all the buttons done up this time. Just like my mother.

I wasn't freaking out. Not at all.

46

SILAS

KNOWING Eve was here in town with me made all the difference in my meetings. I'd wanted to climb back in bed with her, do some of that multitasking pussy eating I'd done at the inn again. The dreaded dinner with the Hyports was now going to be pleasant because I had my wife by my side. I was eager to show her off, let them see how amazing she was. Independent, feisty, and had the same business savvy that I did and without the CEO father or hints of nepotism to get in her way.

With June manning Steaming Hotties back in Hunter Valley, Eve had a day of leisure. So far, she'd slept in. A massage, some shopping would be relaxing. She'd earned it because she worked too hard.

I was at my desk in the office given to me to use while in the Hyport building. I wasn't on the top floor or anywhere near a corner office, but the view of the bay was impressive. If it wasn't so cloudy, I would be able to see the Golden Gate Bridge.

Bradley knocked on the open door, then came in. "I have the information you wanted."

Where I was fair, with blond hair and pale eyes, my assistant's skin was the shade of Eve's darkest roast coffee, his black hair trimmed close to his head. He was in a crisp gray suit and had a file tucked under his arm.

I smiled grimly at what he'd uncovered. Eve had easily distracted me on the plane from the details of her ex. A man was only so strong. But I needed to know.

"Tell me."

He flipped the folder open.

I settled into the high-backed desk chair and listened.

"Cheney Douglas IV. Thirty. Grew up outside of Hunter Valley, skipped college to return to the family business. Parents are Cheney Douglas III and Enid Custer Douglas. Only child. The Douglas's had the original claim on the DouglasGrove Mine back in the 1800s. Back then it was gold, but now they mine hard rock."

"Meaning..."

He looked up from the report, met my gaze. "Meaning they gut the land for rock which is crushed and used for commercial and construction projects around the west."

"Right. I read something about them from the land search for the James Inn. Go on," I prodded, grabbing a stapler and fiddling with it.

"Parents don't work. Just like Eve Hunter's parents. They live off the gains of their predecessors."

Mav, Theo, Dex, and I were all descendants of James family members who made a fortune but we didn't kick back and do nothing. I'd go apeshit if I sat around and did nothing. So would the others. That didn't mean I wanted to work remotely all over the world for the rest of my life either.

"Douglas is listed as CFO of the corporation, but I have yet to find proof of him accomplishing anything."

I set the stapler down, lined it up so it was parallel to the desk phone. "No college or MBA and he's the chief financial officer of a huge mine?"

That seemed far-fetched. Or nepotism. Or both.

He nodded. "Correct."

"You're saving the best for last," I guessed.

"I don't have all the details yet, but the parents–the Douglas and Hunter families–are friends through the country club. Known each other for years. In their circles, it's not news that Cheney Douglas and Evelyn Hunter have been an item for years."

I nodded. "Eve mentioned that. This sounds like an

arranged marriage to me. The question is... why? Especially after years. Five, six, seven years. That's fucking ridiculous. Something's going on."

I hated thinking that Eve had been dealing with her parents and Douglas pestering her all alone, especially the way Douglas showed up at the coffee shop the day before with the sole intention of harassing her. No, there was no intention. They were fucking with her and her livelihood. Not fair and a dick move. She was too close to it, to her parents even though they got her into this, to understand the depth of their reasoning. It wasn't a religious thing. Or a cultural thing. It was something else and it couldn't be good.

"I mean, I could see her father telling her he wasn't giving her more money from her trust, but why make Douglas executor?" I wondered. Everything he shared validated what Eve told me on the plane last night. I'd been admittedly, and amazingly, distracted.

If those fuckers were up to something, which I was sure they were, I wanted to know because they were fucking with my wife.

Her money challenges didn't matter any longer. She had all the money she wanted. Not because she now supposedly had access to her trust fund, but because she was now Eve James. There was no prenup, so she was now a billionaire. A stupid move perhaps on my part, but I didn't give a shit.

I knew for a fact that Dex hadn't had a prenup with Lindy. Sure, they'd been drunk and got hitched at a drive-thru chapel in Las Vegas, but he'd planned to marry her since the second he laid eyes on her. Not only did he have family money, but he made millions as a pro hockey player. He didn't give a shit either.

Bradley gave a shrug. "I've got investigators looking into financials. Digital paper trails. Everything."

"Good. Thanks."

He shut the folder and looked me in the eye. "Want to update me on why your agenda for today includes dinner with Mr. and Mrs. Hyport... and your wife?"

47

EVE

MR. HYPORT OPENED the front door of his home himself considering the place was fancy enough for a butler. Or two. From the street, it was three stories, stucco, consistent with turn of the century San Francisco architecture. This street, specifically their side, rested on a cliff above the bay.

"Welcome!" he said, a broad smile on his face. The man was in his sixties, dressed in dark corduroys and a checked button-up shirt. Sharp eyes met mine, but they held warmth.

With Silas at my side and his hand on the small of my back, he ushered us inside.

"Remember, I'm getting you naked after this," he whispered in my ear as Mr. Hyport took our coats.

I shivered and pasted a smile on my face. I couldn't believe he said that to me.

Now.

Except maybe not.

We met in the hotel lobby as planned. When he saw me, he stopped in his tracks and looked me over, from my black heels to the top of my as-best-as-I-could styled hair.

"Fuck, you're gorgeous," he'd said, cupping my cheek and kissing me. Lavishly, right there in the middle of the lobby.

"Silas," I'd whispered, a little embarrassed by his blatant show of affection.

He pulled back, but only slightly. "What? Now you don't want people to see us?"

I blushed as he continued. "See that couch over there?" He pointed to one with a potted palm beside it. "I want to bend you over it and fuck you, make everyone eyeing my beautiful wife know that she's all mine. That I'm the one who will satisfy her. Make her scream."

Yeah, he'd said that, then led me to a waiting car. Panties wet. Nipples hard. Horny.

"My wife, Eve," Silas said, introducing me to Mr. Hyport.

"Sir, nice to meet you," I said when he took my hand next.

"Robert. Ah, here's Kathleen."

He turned at his wife's approach.

I had gone shopping for a dinner outfit because I'd had no choice. I'd had to wash my panties in the sink and use the hairdryer on them to be able to leave the room. The concierge directed me to an amazing shopping area, and I'd found a few casual items to hold me over, but also the dress and heels I wore now.

I didn't really like my mother very much, but I had to admit, she prepared me well for a moment like this. I knew the outfit required to meet a corporate CEO and I'd bought it. With my own money.

"I'm so glad you're both here," she replied. In a pair of black pants and a white blouse–untucked–she looked effortless and casual. Her hair fell to her shoulders in a sleek, simple style. She wore thick black glasses like Bridget's. She gave off a warm, effortless air and I liked her immediately. "Robert has been so busy with this deal that I haven't seen him as much as I like. I'm sure you feel the same way," she said to me.

I nodded, although I was suddenly unsure of myself. What did they think of me? That I was a horny hussy who did video sex with her husband while he was out of town?

"It smells amazing. Is that... garlic bread?" I asked, falling back on compliments.

She grinned. "You have a good nose. Yes, along with lasagna."

"Kathleen is an amazing cook," Robert said, patting his stomach. While I wouldn't say he had washboard abs beneath his shirt, he was fit for his age.

"He married me for my pasta," she said, glancing fondly at her husband.

"Is there anything I can help you with?" I asked.

She came over, hooked my arm in hers and led me deeper into the house. "You can put ice in the glasses while I make the salad dressing. While we do, you must tell me where you found those wonderful earrings."

I glanced over my shoulder at Silas, who winked.

The kitchen was as big and shiny and amazing as I expected, but I didn't pay it too much attention. I went to the floor to ceiling windows and looked out. The light was fading fast on the stunning view of the water and the cliffs and the focal point, the Golden Gate Bridge. The mountains were spectacular in Hunter Valley, but this? The bridge was amazing the way it glowed red in the distance, that–

"I never get tired of the view," Kathleen said from somewhere behind me. "We bought this house thirty-five years ago. You should have seen it then." She laughed, clearly remembering. "There was a raccoon family living on the second floor."

I turned, wide eyed. "Did you kick them out?"

She was at the counter with the things she needed for her dressing spread out.

"I should say we have a guest bedroom for them, but one look at me and Robert and they fled."

I joined her at the counter. "Oh, the ice."

She pointed to a tray with goblets and then the fridge with a built-in icemaker.

"That was a long time ago. We've had five children since then and four of them have children."

I carried the tray and set it next to the fridge, glanced at her over my shoulder. "You are good examples for them."

She cocked her head, smiled, as she held a bottle of olive oil. "I hope so. You and Silas are just starting your lives together. What fun."

I nodded, then pressed one glass into the dispenser for ice.

When I traded glasses, she continued. "I've met Silas a few times. He's such a nice man. And handsome."

I grinned. Blushed. "I think so."

"That's important, too. The heat."

I filled another glass.

"You two met when he visited his brothers in Montana."

"That's right."

"Silas also tells us–"

"He's told you quite a bit," I said, surprised.

She pushed her glasses up. "Of course he has. Especially about you and that you run a coffee shop! What hard work."

"Yes, it's called Steaming Hotties."

Her eyes sparkled and she pointed a garlic press at me. "I love it! What fun. Tell me more."

So I told her as I filled the other two glasses, then leaned against the counter and watched as she pulled together a vinaigrette, then poured it over a salad in a large wooden bowl.

"Pink t-shirts?" she asked. "Oh, I must have one."

"You want to wear one of my shirts?" I asked, completely surprised.

She tucked her hair behind her ear, then went to the wall oven to peek inside.

"Why wouldn't I?"

She grabbed oven mitts and pulled out a tray with garlic bread.

"Well, um…"

I didn't want to tell her my mother wouldn't be caught dead in a t-shirt, my store or not, and definitely not a pink one.

She set the tray on a wooden cutting board, then yanked off the mitts.

"You will send me one, and for my two daughters as well. The perfect stocking stuffers for next month, don't you think?"

I could only nod because my throat was clogged with tears. Ridiculous, but she wanted my t-shirts. She was interested in my shop. She was interested in me, just as I was.

The men came in then, Silas coming to my side and kissing the top of my head. "Okay?" he asked.

"Yeah."

"That tray of lasagna has been sitting there for thirty minutes. Don't make me wait any longer," Robert said, going to it and peeking beneath the foil.

Kathleen laughed and smacked his hand, then passed him the oven mitts. "It had to rest."

He carried the dish to the table and said, "Eat your fill, Silas. When Kathleen cooks, I'm on dish duty and you will be too since your wife helped. This happens every night because I can't cook."

"I'll have you, Eve, make the coffee later since you're the expert," Kathleen said.

"Eve told you about her shop?" Silas asked Kathleen. It seemed he wanted to make sure the woman knew about me and my business.

"Oh yes. She's sending me a t-shirt."

Silas laughed. "My brother wears one. I think it's his favorite shirt. You should see the place, Robert. It's busy

all the time. Eve's made a deal to stock the James Inn in
Hunter Valley and we hope to add the other inns around
the country next year."

I blinked. We did?

"Impressive," Robert added, giving me a smile that
only looked... proud. He took a slice of garlic bread and
passed the plate to Silas.

"We'll need to work with the distributor for a larger
supply, but Eve has plans with them in Costa Rica."

"Maybe another honeymoon. I'm sure after the blizzard you just had you'd like somewhere warm," Kathleen
suggested, using a spatula to put a huge portion of
lasagna on a plate and handing it to Silas.

"Good thinking," he replied. "We can go there and–"

"No more talking business at the table," Kathleen
advised, plating another section of lasagna. "Although I
thought I'd have to warn you two off about the buyout,
not Eve cornering the coffee market."

Cornering the coffee market? With a huge smile,
Kathleen handed me the plate and I set it in front of me.

What was happening? Did Silas say *we*? That we'll
need to work with the distributor? That we hope to add
other inns?

We?

Steaming Hotties was mine. My shop. My dream.

But now, it was Silas's, too?

Oh shit. It was. When we married, Steaming Hotties belonged to him as well.

What had I done? I needed him as my husband to get control of my trust, but I obviously hadn't thought that through. Not with Cheney pestering me. Now he had control of my business, which was something Cheney never had. Steaming Hotties was small. Barely making a profit. Yet he had plans for it. Big ones, based off the way he was talking.

Was he taking it over, just like he was Hyport Hotels?

Oh God. Had I let another man take control?

48

SILAS

DINNER with the Hyports went well. Eve seemed to enjoy herself, especially since Kathleen seemed to have taken her under her wing. They even shared phone numbers to catch up about sending the pink t-shirts. No talk about business had been allowed, although I'd been able to slip in how proud I was of Eve. I'd dealt in hotels for so long, a coffee shop was so different. Sure, it was still within the hospitality industry, but the scale and the opportunities that were out there for Eve were amazing.

Back at the hotel, I'd gotten Eve naked, just as promised. I took her not once, but twice, then again early this morning.

The final touches on the contract with Hyport were

in the works and the deal would be complete in the next few days. Eve was no longer needed in town–the Hyports loved her most likely more than me. I had no doubts she was anxious to get back to the shop. Her friend June had been running it for her, but as CEO, I knew it wasn't the same for her as being there and in control herself.

The jet was scheduled to take her back to Hunter Valley and I wasn't thrilled. I wanted her here with me. Naked. Screaming my name. Mine and only mine.

I didn't want to talk with her on the phone. Or have video sex with her like Dex had suggested, even though I knew we were really fucking good at it. I was getting grumpier by the minute and she hadn't even left town yet.

"Hi."

I looked up from my paperwork and there she was in the doorway. In those awesome jeans with the hole in the knee. I popped to my feet and came around to her.

"Hey, kitten."

Nothing was going to stop me from kissing her. Her mouth was soft and sweet and mine.

Her eyes were wide and full of glassy-eyed need. It'd only been a few hours, but I wanted her again. "Fuck, I can't get enough of you."

"That's what got us into this mess in the first place," she reminded.

"I like this mess," I said with a final kiss and a sigh.

"The deal should be done tomorrow or the next day. Then I'll be back in Hunter Valley. Until then, I want you to video chat me tonight."

Her eyes widened.

"I'll be in my hotel room. No cam room. Just my phone and your phone. Dex approved."

She laughed. "I'm not sure if I want to know why your brother approves of our sexy times."

I snagged her again, cupped her waist. "Mmm, sexy times."

"You're insatiable," she replied.

"I'm not the only one," I countered, noticing that her nipples poked against her top. Fuck, I wished I could shut my office door and have my way with her.

"I wanted to say goodbye," she said.

"I'm glad you did. In fact, I have some papers for you to sign before you go." I went around the desk to the folder Bradley had dropped off a little earlier from the lawyers. Now she'd know, before she went back to Montana, how serious I was about us. That while the marriage had been to make Hyport happy, I was the one who was so fucking satisfied. Content. Hell, in love. "I was going to bring them with me to Hunter Valley, but we can do it now."

"Papers?"

I looked up from my shuffling. "Yes. Now that you're Mrs. James, these are all standard."

She blinked. "Oh. Right. A prenup."

I frowned. Prenup? That would have happened before a wedding, not after. "No, this is a contract with the James Inn San Juan to handle the coffee. Just a formality after the deal with Mav. Then this one"–I held up a different contract–"is for the warehouse in Costa Rica." I rearranged the pile to find the one I was looking for. The one that gave her the deed to my apartment in Denver. I had no clue where she lived in Hunter Valley, something I needed to fix, but I wanted her to know she was mine and that I would come home to her. That it wasn't my place in Denver, but ours. "Ah. This one. This one gives you–"

"Wait." She held up her hands as if stopping traffic. "Wait. The warehouse in Costa Rica?"

I grinned, excited. "Yes, for us to get the coffee distributors to–"

The look on her face was not as expected. She didn't look thrilled, she looked horrified. "Silas. No. Stop. Enough."

49

EVE

OH MY GOD! I started to pace his office. What had I done? Holy shit.

"No?" Silas asked. "Kitten, what's the matter?"

I spun around, sliced my hand through the air. "Don't kitten me. God, Silas, this was supposed to be to help each other. Get you out of your jam with the deal. Me to get my trust."

"Right." I wasn't understanding the problem.

"It's not that now! Don't you see? You said *we*."

"Okay."

"We will work on the other inn and the coffee supply. We will work with the Costa Rica distributors. Are you going to help with the Hunter Valley store too?"

"I had a handyman drop by to fix the sink and the other things on the list."

"You fixed the sink?" I said, running a hand over my hair. "You really did that? I was doing that! I was doing it all. Then you stepped in and are taking it all away from me."

"You really want to fix the dripping sink?"

I looked up finally, glared at him.

He ran a hand over his beard. "I'm not taking anything away from you."

"You got a deal with the coffee distributors." I set my hand on my chest. "*My* distributors."

He shrugged, as if it wasn't a big deal. "Well, it wasn't hard to have my people track them down. I know they're thrilled about the changes."

"Changes? You didn't talk to me about the changes. You didn't talk to me about the San Juan inn deal."

"But–"

"No!" I shouted. "I should have known you'd take over. God. All you wanted from me was these deals. These chances to make more money."

He came around the desk slowly, as if afraid to make me more freaked out. That was impossible. I was practically shaking with anger and frustration.

"That's not true."

"All I am is arm candy. God, you gave me your credit card and patted me on the head to find a cute outfit while you make deals with my Costa Rican contacts."

"You said you needed clothes."

"Because we left Hunter Valley without me packing!" I tossed my arms up in the air. "I have clothes. Clothes that are really me, not the dress I bought to look like the proper CEO wife. I have my business, Silas. I have my trust. I don't need you."

"Kitten."

I blanched, put my fingers to my lips. "Don't... don't take away Steaming Hotties."

Tears filled my eyes, and I didn't see him step right in front of me. He set his hands on my hips. "I wouldn't."

I shook my head and a tear slipped down my cheek. "You already have. You have the power here. You said you had people working on growing the business. In less than two days, you've already got control of my coffee bean distributors. You had lawyers draw up contracts for God knows what else. We're married. You can take it all away."

"You need to calm down."

"Calm down?" I shouted, then started to pace. "I can't calm down. I was so stupid. I cammed instead of taking the loan. I should have taken it and then none of this would have happened." I spun away, shook my head. "I'm an idiot. Why do I always do this? As if getting married was going to solve everything. A fake marriage got me my trust fund back, but you'll just take the business."

"I'm not taking your business!" he practically shouted. "As for fake, there's nothing fake about how I feel about you."

"Our marriage isn't real, Silas."

"It's real," he growled.

"It's based on money, just like every other relationship in my life. My parents, they don't love each other. They stick together because of greed. My mother dresses me and wants me to play along to whatever the menfolk say, regardless of what I want. *Be a good girl, wear my pearls and get a massage.* She's never once heard me. My father doesn't give a shit about me, only that I, again, fall in line and that's for me to be married to Cheney. And Cheney, he doesn't love me. He wants me as arm candy. Oh, and my money. To try and take control. To stop him, I *married* you." I shook my head, refusing to look at him. "Turned out, it wasn't control I got. While I made the choice to marry for money, I don't want it. It was never really about the money."

"Kitten, fuck. No."

I was outright crying now, and I swiped angrily at my face. "We got what we wanted. You, the deal. Me, the trust fund. I didn't beg Cheney when he had power over me, but I'm begging you, as my husband. Leave me and Steaming Hotties alone."

I ran out of the room, ignoring when Silas called my name.

50

SILAS

W<small>HAT THE FUCK JUST HAPPENED</small>?

I wanted her for her money? That I would take Steaming Hotties from her?

Shit. Shit! I needed to make this right.

I took off after her but didn't make it ten feet past the office door.

"Silas."

I stopped, turned. "Mr. Hyport."

He stood there, hands in his pants pockets. Shit. How much had he heard?

"Son, I think we need to have a talk."

All of it. He heard the whole thing.

51

EVE

"WHY ISN'T Theo helping with this?" Bridget asked Mallory, cutting out probably her hundredth feather.

I was at Mallory's house, down the street from mine. Bridget got wrangled into helping Mallory cut up construction paper pieces of turkeys for her first graders' Thanksgiving craft projects. And since she got wrangled, she got me involved. She called me a few hours after I got home and buried myself in my bed to wallow in self-pity. Told me Bradley called her and said I was home and that I needed wine.

To Bridget, that didn't mean the bar or a girls' night with a box of red and a carton of ice cream. It meant I had a pile of red construction paper in front of me and I was in charge of cutting those wobbly turkey jowls. Mallory said the real term was a wattle, but they were jowls to me.

I didn't really care. I didn't care my face was splotchy or that I was in the sweats I wore when I cleaned my house. I didn't care about anything.

"I mean, he's a surgeon and should be talented with scissors."

"Actually, he sucks at scissors," Mallory replied, then paused in her turkey body cutting. "I should get a scalpel for him and he can cut them that way on a cutting board. I bet his feathers would be precise."

"That means we can stop?" Bridget asked, another leaf falling into her pile of brown ones.

"No. These need to be done for tomorrow and Theo's off with Mav. Don't worry, Hanukkah's coming and he'll be doing all the candles for the menorahs in a few weeks."

They'd been like this since I arrived, talking about ridiculous things, anything besides the huge elephant in the room. Me and Silas. I knew it was coming. Hell, I was impressed they made it this long.

We cut for a minute or so in silence before Mallory piped up.

"So Eve," she began, grabbing another piece of paper. "Bridge filled me in on your double life."

I stopped mid-cut and stared.

"Your cam job?" Mallory grinned. "It's awesome! I could connect you with my friends Trixie and Annie. They're call girls in Vegas and could give you some pointers."

My mouth fell open because not only was that a surprise, but she mentioned having call girls as friends with a surprising casualness.

"Thanks," I said. "But I quit." It was such old news now.

"Oh? That's a bummer. I mean, reading sex scenes is genius. You could do that forever."

Mallory put down her scissors and grabbed the box of wine and topped off my glass.

"It was Silas who bought up her time," Bridget told Mallory.

"What?" Mallory asked. She didn't seem easily stunned, but this worked. "That's really hot."

The mention of him hurt. I shook my head. "He paid for me. It's not that hot after all because it was about him wanting to give me money. Nothing more."

"That's not true," Bridget countered softly.

I gave her a look and she didn't say more because she knew I was right.

"It was Silas she got snowed in with at the inn," Bridget reminded Mallory. "He went there because he's totally in love with her and couldn't handle her camming."

"He's not in love with me," I said, but Mallory's eyes lit up like Bridget told her she'd get free coffee for life.

"I heard! Oh my God, to be snowed in together?"

Clearly the two of them were talking about me as if I wasn't in the room.

Bridget nodded. "Silas told Mav to wait two days to have the plows do the driveway. I think it's romantic. How often could he be stuck somewhere with you with the perfect excuse not to be able to work?"

I looked at my paper jowl. "Wait. Silas really said not to send the plows?"

Bridget nodded, which made her push her glasses up.

Me and Silas being stuck together at the inn wasn't orchestrated. He'd showed up like Bridget said because I'd riled him to the point of turning into a caveman, but he couldn't have coordinated a snowstorm where we'd be stuck together, no matter how much money he had to throw at it. But he could force us to stay together longer without a way to leave. I was pretty sure Silas didn't plan on licking chocolate sauce off my body either, although he may have fantasized about it.

I swiped at a tear, then another.

Bridget crawled over the pieces of paper strewn on the floor and hugged me. "What did he do?"

Mallory stayed quiet and stopped cutting turkey parts.

I sniffled. "He married me."

Bridget pushed me away so fast she gave me whiplash.

Mallory's mouth dropped open.

Nothing was said for five seconds and then–

"What?"

"*Married* you?"

"When?"

"Because of the cam room?"

I grabbed a red turkey feather and used it to wipe my cheeks. "It's a long story."

Mallory grabbed the box of wine again and topped us all off, mine to the very top. "We've got all night and forty-six more turkeys to cut out."

52

SILAS

MY TALK with Robert Hyport didn't happen right away. No, like a child in trouble, I had to wait hours until he had a free moment for me. Which was late that night.

The deal was over. I knew it. He'd overheard the marriage was a fake. That we'd orchestrated it to close the deal. My father may have fucked Hyport's assistant, but he never actually *married* someone to close a deal. The man may have been a womanizing asshole, but he was solid in business.

Me? I got involved in cam room shit during a meeting *and* faked a marriage.

I dreaded the meeting, more because it was delayed than the topic of conversation. I texted Mav and warned him the deal was dead because he was wrong. I wasn't like our father. I was worse.

I wanted to be scolded. Shamed. Told by Hyport I'd disappointed him. Then I wanted to be on a plane back to Denver to sulk in private.

Thankfully, once I sat across from him in his office, Hyport didn't start with small talk. "Please explain what I overheard earlier between you and your wife, if that's what she really is."

53

EVE

"HOLY SUGAR AND SPICE," Mallory said when I told them everything, minus the sex stuff. She made it a habit not to swear since she was a first-grade teacher. She knew if she started, she'd let all the f-bombs and friends drop in her classroom.

"Yeah, holy shit," Bridget added.

"I can't believe he told you to calm down."

I had to laugh at Mallory, because out of everything I shared, from the confrontation with Cheney to the wedding in the police station to the contracts Silas wanted me to sign, that's what she said first.

"Do you really think Silas wants Steaming Hotties?" Bridget asked.

"He had a contract for my coffee to be in the San Juan James Inn location."

Mallory frowned. "What does that have to do with him taking over your shop?"

"He talked with the distributor in Costa Rica about a warehouse," I added.

"It sounds like you're going to need more beans if you're going to be handling another inn."

"At the dinner with the Hyports Silas kept saying *we* and talking about all the things we're going to do with the place."

"That sounds like he's behind you all the way."

I tossed my hands up, then took a big swig of my wine. I had no idea how much I drank because Mallory kept refilling it. "With money!" They stared at me. "What?"

"He's a billionaire," Mallory said. "He has money. He's using it because he wants to help you."

I shook my head. "No."

"He loves you," Bridget added. "He never would have married you if he didn't."

"No," I repeated. "He never said it. Not once." I'd have remembered that because no one else had ever said it to me either.

"Well, he's a dumbass," Bridget added.

I shook my head again. "My parents controlled me with money. When I finally started to push back, they made it worse. Cheney got involved. The guy I dated for years used money against me, to force me to do what he wanted."

"Your ex is named *Cheney?*" Mallory asked. "That sounds like an asshole's name."

The corner of my mouth twitched at the way her face looked, all scrunched up as if she smelled something bad.

Bridget reached over, took my hand. "Silas doesn't want your business, I'm sure of it. He wants it to succeed. He's a CEO. It's literally hardwired in him to see businesses thrive."

"Exactly. He needed me to be his wife to ensure his deal went through."

"You had every right to freak out," Mallory said. "I mean, he wanted you to take a spa day on his credit card. What an idiot. But maybe hear the idiot out."

Bridget nodded. "Real love, love I think you have with Silas, what I have with Mav and Mal has with Theo, it's unconditional."

"Theo flew to Vegas to help me out of my hooker arrest because he loved me when he didn't know it."

I stared at her, unsure if what she was saying was an exaggeration or truth. "Hooker arrest?"

She waved me off. "Another long story."

"Your parents love themselves first," Bridget continued. "Same thing with your ex. I have a feeling, if you hear him out, you may see that he's been thinking of you all along."

"Does that make me the asshole then? I mean, I wanted to marry him right back, not because of love, but because it gave me access to my trust."

"You did that because it was the only way to ditch that dead weight you've been carrying. The worst examples of love around."

"I don't know what love is then," I admitted.

Bridget gave me a soft smile. "You do. You love Silas. You loved him all while you thought it was conditional."

I frowned. "How do you know?"

"Yeah, how do you know, Yoda?" Mallory asked Bridget.

"Because your heart is broken right now. If you didn't love him, you wouldn't hurt."

Bridget's cell pinged with a text. She grabbed it and her face fell.

"What?" Mallory said. "What's the matter?"

"It's from Mav. Silas texted him." Bridget looked my way, then held her phone out for me to read.

Hyport deal is dead. I'm worse
than Dad.

I gasped at what Silas sent Mav. From what he told me about his father, Silas was *nothing* like him. So what if he watched porn during a business meeting. So what if he faked a marriage to close a deal. He didn't screw people over.

I gasped again at what came to me.

He didn't screw people over.

Silas wouldn't screw me over. He had only wanted to help me, and I'd shut him down with every chance.

I had to fix this. I was the only one. I knew just who to call.

54

SILAS

"It all started with the cam room?" Robert asked.

I came clean with the man. All of it, although I left out all the sex, which made my recount pretty short. I also skipped what Eve did in the cam room, but I wouldn't shame her that way. Although, I had a feeling he knew, or at least the gist, since he'd overheard a few naughty seconds of it.

I shook my head. "It started with Eve turning down the James Corp loan."

"The program your brother and his future wife created."

I nodded. "That's correct. And it ended with us marrying. For me to ensure this deal went through and for her to get control of her trust fund. We married for money."

He made a sound, like a grunt of disappointment.

"Except for the date of our wedding, every aspect of our James/Hyport deal, every aspect of our... friendship is the truth."

I wasn't sure if he saw me as a friend, but I considered him one. A mentor, in a sense. He'd started his hotel empire before I was born. I only took over mine. Now that he was retiring, I had hoped to do him proud with where I could take his hotels into the future.

But not now.

"I'm not sure if I could make a story like that up if I wanted to lie," I admitted.

"What happens with her ex?" he asked. "The man who controls... controlled her trust?"

I couldn't imagine why that was so important in all of this, but he had me by the balls.

"I've dug up some information on him. Shady sh– stuff." I shifted in my seat. "There's more, I'm sure. I'll get it soon and see him ruined."

He nodded. "Good."

I sighed, met his shrewd gaze. "I know the deal is dead," I said, resigned to it. "I have too much respect for you to expect to continue a working relationship. You were right to end things with my father and you're right to end things now."

"And if I want the deal to go through?" he wondered, studying me closely.

The answer was easy. "I'd end it myself."

"Oh?"

I nodded, shifting in my chair. "Like I said, I'm just like my father. Maybe worse."

I glanced at my hands.

He was quiet and I let him take the time he wanted. Filling it with empty chatter was a sign of nervousness. Of weakness. I was neither. I was resolved. After all these years since my father died, after all this time busting my ass to prove I was nothing like my old man, I finally caught on that I couldn't run away from fate.

Finally, Robert spoke. "You forget I knew your father. Very well."

I nodded, but I hadn't forgotten. That was why it seemed I'd worked extra hard on this deal.

"You didn't marry Eve for money," he said.

I looked up, met his gaze. "What?"

"You married her because you didn't want to let me down."

I stared at him, tried to understand what the hell he was talking about. "What?" I asked again, eventually.

"Your father was no role model. Or maybe he was for you, but in what *not* to do. What not to be in a CEO. Because of this, or despite him, you've turned into an incredible leader. You have every value a corporation like the James Hotels needs. And Hyport as well.

I blinked at him. Confused. "Um... what?"

He smiled.

Smiled?

"Silas, I'm proud of you."

My mouth fell open and I stared. And stared some more. The words sunk in and... shit. I looked away. Emotion clogged my throat. Hopping to my feet, I paced his office.

"You've never heard that before, have you?"

I shook my head hard but couldn't face him.

"I've watched you for years. Followed how you turned James Corp around. How you grew it. Did everything you're supposed to do. That was why I wanted to sell to you."

I spun and faced him again.

I ran a hand over my neck. "Because you're proud of me? That makes no sense."

"To you, probably not. If you want to end this deal because of marrying Eve, you're dumber than I thought."

My eyes widened, stunned. "Why's that?"

"Because I know a good man when I see one."

He stood, came around the desk and set his hand on my shoulder. "Because you're not anything like your father. You never were."

I shook my head.

"You doubt me?" he continued. "Believe your wife."

I blinked, wiped my nose. "Eve?"

He nodded. "She called Kathleen earlier. Told her she wouldn't give any pink coffee shop t-shirts to anyone who weren't on Team Silas. Those are her words, not mine. Oh, and she offered a two-million-dollar incentive to the sale."

"WHAT?" I shouted.

He nodded. "That wife of yours offered up her trust fund to sweeten the deal."

I laughed, the long-lingering pain of my father sliding away. That feeling was replaced by what I felt for Eve. She would give up her trust fund for me? For the deal? That money wouldn't cover the price of linens, but it was a sign. A sign she loved me unconditionally. That she'd walk away from what she'd fought so hard for.

For me.

Shit. SHIT!

"I blew it with her. That's why she stormed out earlier," I told him, scrubbing the back of my neck.

He stepped back, shook his head. "Son, there's nothing fake about your marriage. You just have a lot to learn about women. For one, never tell a woman to calm down."

55

EVE

I CALLED Kathleen and told her everything. Told her that it was all my fault, the deal falling through, that I was a horrible fake wife. I also told her that the man who was at her house the other night for dinner was the real Silas. Honest. Kind. Funny. Caring. I left out sexy, but she was a woman and she had eyes.

While I didn't hold the Steaming Hotties t-shirts for her and her daughters hostage, I pretty much implied that I didn't give them to those who couldn't see Silas was the real deal. And that extended to her husband, too.

If Mr. Hyport needed a little incentive, I offered my trust fund to sweeten the pot. While I needed the money to keep the coffee shop going, getting a hold of it had never really been about that all along. It had been about taking charge of what was mine. Of being free from my father–and then Cheney–who never gave me value. Who never cared for me.

When Kathleen told me the deal was worth billions, I felt like a fool for my measly add-on.

After I hung up, I knew I'd been right to offer it. Silas deserved the Hyport deal. Deep down I knew he really wasn't like Cheney and my father. Or his. He didn't screw people over.

We were very similar, Silas and I. We never knew what real love was until it pretty much kicked us in the teeth.

And now I was alone. I had my money. I had exactly what I'd wanted all along and I didn't care. I'd accused Silas of some pretty mean things. I definitely hit one of his triggers and I didn't blame him if he hated me.

It hurt like hell, but it was my own stupid fault. It was time to get my own shit together. To face my parents and let go once and for all.

That was why when my mother texted reminding me of the party and that pearls would look best with the green velvet, I decided to go. I wasn't caught up with hope that my parents would be anything but what they were. That Cheney would be anything besides a dick.

I was in my bedroom, staring at the velvet dress my

mother brought over. I'd slung it over the back of the chair in my bedroom and forgotten about it.

The dress was beautiful, but not me. It was stuffy. Fancy. And I didn't think I could ever wear pearls again. I turned from it and went to my closet. She bought it with the intention of me wearing it for Cheney. No, *with* Cheney. I could only imagine what a green velvet tie looked like if he had one that matched. Maybe it was just the same shade of green. Or plaid. Or...

Who cared? Not me.

I was married, without a husband. I needed to reinforce with Cheney, and my parents... and everyone at the country club, that I'd moved on from them. That I wasn't under my parents' control. Or Cheney's. That I wasn't closing Steaming Hotties.

I had to make a stand finally.

I grabbed a black sequin jumpsuit I bought on clearance from an online shop. I'd loved it in the catalog and bought it last year on a whim. I'd never worn it, but this was the perfect time.

I slipped it on, worked the zipper up in the back and stood in front of the mirror.

Smiled.

I loved it. The high neck, the slight puff to the sleeves, the straight legs. Hell, it had pockets.

It was dressy, but fun.

My mother was going to hate it because it was pants. PANTS at a party. And sequins. God forbid!

I couldn't help but grin.

I found black heels and accessorized with gold hoop earrings and bright red lipstick.

Forty-five minutes later, when I handed my keys to the valet at the club, I lost a little bit of my nerve and, after getting my ticket from coat check, ducked into the ladies' room. Stared at myself in the mirror, just like I had forever ago when I went for the interview for the James Corp loan.

I laughed to myself. Where would I be now if I'd just taken that money? If I hadn't put a financial value on love?

"There you are," my mother said, poking her head into the bathroom, then did a double take. "What *are* you wearing?"

And just like that, I was fine. Better than fine. I saw my mother clearer now. Compared her to Kathleen and how she'd welcomed me into her home. Had me fill glasses with ice within five minutes as if I wasn't a guest, but an old friend.

I rolled my shoulders back. "You look lovely, Mother. That color suits you."

She stepped back to let me exit the bathroom, then guided me toward the party. The sounds of voices and music, the scent of roasting meat carried down the hall.

"What is this about you being married? Cheney mentioned it the other day and I couldn't imagine he was correct."

I pasted on a smile. "It's true. I did get married. Where's Father? I assume Cheney is with him."

Not waiting for a response, I headed into the hall and grabbed a glass of wine off a tray carried by a passing waiter.

My mother caught up and then my father and Cheney appeared, like two vultures swooping down.

"Father, Cheney, how's the scotch?" I asked. I didn't want to say they looked well or ask them how they were doing.

They stood side by side, my father in a charcoal suit and Cheney in a black one with... yeah, a green velvet tie just like the dress.

"You're really married?" my mother wondered. "But Cheney–"

"If Cheney still thinks he has a chance with me, then he's an idiot." I gave him a pointed look, then down at the tie. All of them still believed we were together even after Cheney met Silas and we told him we were married. The guy had either hit his head or really was an idiot. "I was out of town, but now that I'm back, I'll ensure my lawyer connects with you about my trust."

"Where is this husband of yours, Evelyn?" Cheney asked, glancing around. Out of all the things he said and all the things he *could* say, this was the sharpest arrow. As if he knew Silas was my weakness.

He was. Because I ruined it. My own insecurities had come out in a ruthless rush. The three people standing in front of me had made me question him. Doubt him. They made me never know what love really was. Silas had and I'd tossed it back at him like a cheap, worthless gift.

I swallowed hard, knowing Cheney wasn't done with his barbs. Why had I come? Why had I shown up? My lawyer could handle the trust. It was literally paperwork that shifted my trust's control into my hands.

"Did he drop you so soon?" Cheney pushed. "I mean, you own a *coffee shop*. I'd think the man would–"

"–apologize for being late," a deep voice said from behind me.

A hand settled on my hip and as a kiss settled on my head. I startled and a little gasp escaped.

I knew that voice. I knew that touch. And the kiss.

Silas. He was here.

56

SILAS

I KNEW COUNTRY CLUB PARTIES. I could read this crowd because I grew up with it. My father had thrived in this fake, gilded, and exclusive world. About a hundred people mingled and chatted with wine and whiskey in hand. A string quartet played Bach from a discreet corner. Waiters in stiff uniforms circled with trays of bacon wrapped scallops and filet on toast tips.

My brothers and I shunned this kind of formal misery. Even in a laid-back town like Hunter Valley, there were still pockets of stuck-up elite. Money didn't keep anyone from being an asshole. Like our father being a dick and needing to be the center of attention in a crowd he'd specifically selected. We didn't need a therapist to pull that out of our subconscious thoughts.

If it weren't for my need to be by Eve's side–my *wife's* side–I'd turn around and leave. Stop at the bar downtown and kick back. Have a few drinks. Play some pool. Fuck my woman over a desk in the back office again.

She had reason to hate this crowd, starting with the couple standing with her and Douglas. Eve's parents. No question.

There was a resemblance between Eve and her mother. The same coloring. The eyes. But Mrs. Hunter was all veneer. Shiny and bright on the outside. I had to wonder if she was vicious and conniving or just dumb on the inside.

The answer would soon become obvious.

I spotted Eve immediately. She didn't want to be here. From across the room, I saw. Could read her misery. Feel it, even.

Yet she practically sparkled with the way the sequins caught the light. Her outfit was modest but sexy-as-fuck. Unlike in the cam room where her curves were flaunted, her pant... outfit showed off every curve I knew by heart but revealed barely any skin. In a sea of plain and boring, she was stunning.

It was clear her mother hated it by the pruned-up look on her face and the way she stared.

"Sorry I'm late. You look perfect," I commented, cutting off anything the woman might say. I'd never seen Eve wear much makeup or have her hair styled. She could polish herself up well, like dinner with the Hyports, but I knew what she looked like with her hair tangled in only my shirt. I was eager to muss her up later if she'd let me. Smear that lipstick and see it coating my dick.

But not yet. She could only be here for one purpose, to finally be done with her ex and deal with her father once and for all. Good, because I was here to help. She'd stood by me. It was time for me to stand by her. To show her that I'd always be at her side. I'd always support her. Love her.

She reached across her body and set her hand on top of mine. Squeezed. I felt the desperation and I was going to take it all away.

As for Vance Hunter, who loomed tall and broody, he was truly an asshole through and through. And desperate. With his always perfect timing, Bradley had shared the damning information I'd been waiting for and I'd gone through it on the flight. It had been illuminating and made me really fucking furious.

"Father, Mother," Eve said. She cleared her throat and lifted her chin. "This is Silas James, my husband."

"Ma'am," I said, tipping my head to Mrs. Hunter first before offering my hand to Eve's father. I didn't like them, not at all, but good manners were ingrained. I wasn't going to stoop to their level. Yet.

Vance Hunter eyed me as we shook. "I've heard quite a bit about you."

"Is that so?" I asked, pulling Eve in closer. The sequins poked into my palm, but I felt her heat. This close, I breathed in her soft scent.

"Silas James?" Her mother's voice was full of surprise. She knew me. Knew *of* me. "You didn't tell me, Evelyn, that your husband is Silas *James*," she murmured, patting Eve on the arm and eyeing me in a calculated way. I was sure she was thinking *good job. A billionaire!*

"That's right, I didn't," Eve commented.

Which meant her father learned it from Douglas. I'd tossed my full name at him in the coffee shop intentionally to see if he'd look into me. He'd taken the bait.

"You two should come for dinner this week," Mrs. Hunter added.

Eve stared at her mother. "Cheney's tie matches the dress you wanted me to wear tonight and now you want me to bring Silas to dinner?"

"Well, I–" she sputtered, but her husband cut her off.

"This marriage is a sham," her father said.

"Don't be so hasty, dear. I mean, he's a *James*." Obviously, Mrs. Hunter had switched allegiance when she learned about the size of my bank account. To her, money was money.

"Mother," Eve scolded. She grabbed my bicep, looked up at me with embarrassed and apologetic eyes.

"Your father's right, Evelyn. Your marriage is a sham." Douglas waved down a waiter and handed off his empty scotch glass as if owned the place. His suit was crisp, his hair was slicked back. He looked like a fucking douche. And he was wearing a velvet tie. What the fuck?

I eyed Eve's father. "I think you're the last one to cast stones, aren't you, Mr. Hunter? I'd say keeping up the façade of your wealth is a sham."

Eve didn't say anything, just looked between us. I offered Eve a reassuring smile. "I had Bradley look into some things. I should have told you, but I take care of what's mine."

I half expected her to jam her high heel into the top of my foot, but she only nodded.

With that, I met her father's narrowed gaze. He knew what was coming and probably had his ass cheeks squeezed tight waiting for me to say it. "Having Douglas here find out about your gambling debts was a big mistake on your part."

Eve's mother gasped and stared up at her husband in horror.

She didn't know. That was what I figured. She was a money-grubbing bitch, but she only wanted what was financially best for her daughter. Above all else.

Vance Hunter? He was worse.

The man clenched his jaw and a vein throbbed in his temple.

"What's Silas talking about?" Eve asked him.

When he didn't respond, I did. "You want to tell your daughter you sold her to Cheney Douglas or do you want me to?"

57

EVE

I TOOK Silas's hand like a life raft. He was what kept me sane, kept me safe. I'd known my father was up to something. Cheney, too. Except I never imagined this. In fact, it was downright crazy. And completely freaking me out.

"That's absurd," my father sputtered, but he was turning an unhealthy shade of purple.

"Is it?" Silas asked. He was as calm as ever. Composed. In his dark suit, he looked amazing. There were dark shadows under his eyes, as if he'd slept as badly as I had, but I was the only one who noticed.

Silas was in his element, and I was thankful for it.

"Those gambling debts were pretty hefty," he continued. "Until Cheney paid them off."

My father looked around, clearly hoping no one else was listening in.

"Vance, what–" my mother began, looking at her husband with surprise and confusion.

"What's wrong with helping out a friend?" Cheney asked, rubbing a hand down his tie.

"When he gives his daughter to the *friend* to marry in exchange for payment, I'd say there's a shit ton wrong," Silas continued.

I blinked. First off, my father gambled? Cheney paid off the debt to marry me? By the look on my mother's face, she had no clue.

"We're not married, so obviously that's a lie," Cheney replied.

"She's married to me," Silas snapped, the possessiveness impossible to miss. It was the first time he showed any heightened emotion. He looked to my father. "As for lying... you didn't expect your daughter to have a mind of her own, did you?" Silas's hand slid up my back to rest on my shoulder. I was tucked into his side now, as close as possible without being in his arms. "Thought she'd give up well before now. Settle down with Cheney and marry. Except she didn't. That's why you made him executor of her trust fund."

WHAT?

I stepped out of Silas's hold, but I wasn't sure if I

should face my father or Cheney. All this was my father's doing, so I got in his face.

"What happened if I didn't marry Cheney?" I asked.

Sweat dotted his temples and his face was now pale. His lips pinched. He wasn't going to say a word.

"Vance, what are they talking about? Gambling? I mean, really," Mother hissed, glancing left and right so no one picked up on the Hunter family drama. It was their party, after all. They wanted to be the center of attention, but not this way.

I kept my gaze squarely on my father. "You've been using me for a long time. All you've wanted me for is money."

It hurt. A lot. I knew my parents' love was conditional. But this was taking it to a whole new level of selfishness and–

"Cheney's bleeding your trust fund dry," Silas said.

I heard his words. Felt them like a knife.

Cheney only smiled. Shrugged. "You wouldn't marry me, so your father owed me something else. The only money left is yours."

My mother gasped. "We're broke? But we're at the country club."

Oh, so my parents were out of money. Not me and my protected trust. I never touched it except to start up Steaming Hotties. Didn't buy fancy cars or live a posh lifestyle. I'd survive without the trust fund, which sounded as if it might be empty because Cheney was a fucking thief. My parents though? My *mother?*

"It wasn't to drive me back to you, you taking over my trust. It was to empty the account," I said to Cheney, finally understanding everything.

Cheney shrugged again, ran his hand down that stupid tie. "You were the prize all along. The Hunter money you offered. Until I learned about your father's debt. Then it all slid into place. Much easier to force someone's hand when they're in over their head. Except for you."

"I was never going to marry you," I spat.

Cheney glanced over my shoulder at Silas. "And I don't take sloppy seconds."

I heard Silas growl. Like a bear. A pissed off bear.

But I wasn't letting him near Cheney. Oh no.

This asshole was mine. I curled my fingers into a fist, reared back and punched him. Hard.

His head rocked back, and I heard his nose break.

"What the fuck!" he shouted, his hands flying up to cover his nose.

He hadn't expected the punch. Why would he? We were at the country club among civilized people. String quartets. Trays of hors d'oeuvres. A woman didn't throw down in the Teton room.

Except I wasn't civilized. Not now. Not when I found out no one in my family ever gave a shit about me. My mother only cared about appearances and her lifestyle. My father was a lying, gambling-addicted asshole who sold off his own daughter. And Cheney? He was scum, willing to marry me to get my bank account.

"Evelyn!" my mother cried.

Now everyone in the room knew shit was going down.

"There are more Hunters than just me and my parents. In fact, one Hunter is the sheriff and he's going to put you in jail," I hissed, breathing hard. My hand hurt, but it was worth it.

Silas stepped close, wrapped an arm around my waist from behind. I wasn't sure if it was to restrain or comfort me. "Nice one, kitten."

The whispered compliment made me smile.

Cheney's face was red, his eyes filled with hatred as blood streamed from his nose and splattered onto his white shirt and the green fucking tie.

"James," Cheney said, looking to Silas and calling him by his last name. "I don't mean Eve's sloppy seconds from you. I mean from all the men she's cammed for."

My mother put her hands on her pearls, clutched them until her knuckles were white.

It was my turn to gasp. How did he know about that?

A sly smile spread across Cheney's face showing bloody teeth. "Yeah, your woman here likes to slum it with random men on the computer. Virgin librarian." He huffed, rolled his eyes. "As if. Wouldn't want you to tarnish the James good name and all of James Corp with a slut like her. CEO of a company whose wife likes to take off her clothes for strangers. That stock's sure to plummet. The deal with Hyport..."

He didn't finish because he made his point quite clear. If he spread the story, it would be bad.

I could ruin Silas and his family. And his company. I knew this because I'd already blown the Hyport Hotel purchase.

Now we had an audience. The entire party stood in a circle around the five of us. Nibbles forgotten. The music had stopped. This was the best gossip the town would have all year and they were witness to it. No doubt someone was recording this with their phone and it would be all over town and the Internet within ten minutes.

"Cheney," I said, begging almost slipping from my lips. Panic set in, my fingers tingling, my heart pounding. I wouldn't see Silas hurt further from me. "How do you know about that?" I whispered. My voice wasn't coming out any louder.

"How else would you get any money? Your trust fund paid for me to do some digging. It wasn't too hard checking out your emails, your computer usage. Direct deposits from a porn chat site."

He'd invaded my privacy. Broke laws. It didn't matter. Not now. Silas was going to–

"Oh, I know all about Eve's screen time," Silas said, calm as a fucking cucumber. I was slowly dying inside of mortification. "It's our thing." Silas winked at Cheney, seemingly proud that now everyone knew we were having sex, and kinky sex at that. "Eve and I. Being watched. Nothing wrong with a little kink in the bedroom, right, kitten?"

He kissed me in front of the entire roomful of people.

Oh my. His lips were soft and gentle while the tight hold on my hip told me and me alone how much he needed me.

When he lifted his head, he didn't look at Cheney as he continued, but met my eyes. Held them. "In fact, so does Mr. Hyport. He was... amused at how my wife and I stay connected when we're apart. As for the deal, the papers are signed. Eve's the proud owner of half of Hyport Hotels."

My mother gasped.

I gasped.

The sale went through.

He did it.

"Ready to get out of here, kitten?"

I blinked, took in his pale eyes. The ones that only saw me. That told me so much.

"She's always wanted the money," Cheney said. "That's all she was ever after."

I'd been after *my* money. I didn't give a shit about Silas's money and he knew that all too well. Silas kept his eyes on me. Waited.

I smiled, turned to Cheney.

"You forget, Cheney. I married Silas for his big dick."

My mother didn't just gasp this time but started coughing.

Looking to Silas, he grinned.

"I'm done."

With a nod, he took my hand. "Then let's get the hell out of here."

58

SILAS

I DIDN'T LET GO of her hand as we left the club. Waiting for the valet, I tugged her into a dark alcove, pressed her up against the wall and kissed her.

It was impossible to wait a second longer. She tipped her head up, her tongue finding mine. Her hands slid under my suit coat and gripped my shirt. My hands cupped her cheeks so I could angle her head and take the kiss deep. Deeper. I was desperate for her, but it couldn't be here.

We came up for air. Eventually. The frigid air swirled around us, but I wasn't the least bit cold. My forehead rested against hers.

"I love you," I said. There was no fucking way I could

wait a second longer to tell her. Because that was what had been missing all along.

She stood up to her parents and her ex. Punched the fucker in the nose. *Now* tears filled her eyes.

"I love you, too."

Those words. Holy shit. I never knew their power. Until now.

"Silas, the deal. I–"

I set a finger on her lips.

"Nothing else matters. Come on."

I led her to my car, which was waiting for us.

"Where are we going?" she asked, looking up at me after I tucked her into the passenger seat.

"My place."

Ten minutes later, I led her into the little miner's shack, kicked the door shut behind us and kissed the hell out of her. Ran my hands over her body, savoring the curves that I'd missed so fucking bad. I pulled back. "How do you get this thing off?"

She laughed, spun around.

"Ah." I worked the zipper down her back, the sequined material parting to reveal her soft skin.

She helped, getting it off her shoulders, down her arms and then it pooled around her ankles. Setting a hand on my arm, she stepped out of it.

"Fuck, kitten."

She was in a black bra with a matching thong. And heels.

"You're wearing too many clothes," she said.

I stripped in record time. If my wife wanted me naked, I'd be fucking naked.

She stared. I stared. She stared some more.

Then jumped me. Literally threw herself into my arms.

I gripped her ass as she wrapped her legs around my waist. Kissed the hell out of me. I heard her heels hit the wood floor as I carried her into the bedroom.

Made her mine. Made her cry out my name as I ate her out.

"Give me that big dick," she said when she came on my mouth and fingers. Her bra was snagged on the headboard and her panties had been ripped to shreds. She was sweaty, relaxed, and perfect.

I crawled up her body, wiped her sticky sweetness from my mouth, settled myself at her entrance.

She gave me a sly, mischievous smile and pushed against my chest. I moved for her, flopping onto my back as she wanted as she came over me.

She gripped me in her small fist. I hissed.

"I want that big dick... in my mouth," she said with the same boldness she had in the cam room. No inhibitions, all need.

I was rock hard, but those words and I throbbed in her hold. "Fuck, kitten."

With her messy hair and flushed skin, she gave me one last sultry look before she took me into her mouth. Destroyed me. Made me whole. Ruined me. Rocked my world. And her lipstick was smeared and all over my dick.

59

EVE

I CAME AWAKE WITH A START, blinking at the ceiling trying to figure out where I was. It was dark out, but the glint of snow made the room bright enough for me to remember.

Silas's.

The country club confrontation.

The sex.

The sex, round two.

The sex, round three.

I smelled coffee.

The door widened and Silas came in, backlit from the lights from the hall.

He was naked.

And a cat circled around his ankles.

"You have a cat?"

He looked down at it, tried to scratch it behind the ears and it bolted, streaking off and I heard a *flip flap* from the other room.

"Sorta. A stray Theo was trying to win over. Even got the guy a cat door."

I couldn't help but grin.

He sat on the edge of the bed and handed me a cup. "What has you eyeing me like that?"

"You're naked."

He looked down at himself. "I'm glad you noticed."

"You're hard."

"Always with you."

"It's a morning thing."

"It's extra hard in the morning with you in my bed," he countered.

I took a sip. "Mmm, that's my coffee."

"It is. There's always a stash of beans in the freezer."

"We didn't talk last night," I said, eyeing him cautiously.

"You want to drink coffee and talk?" he asked. "I liked the other multitasking option better."

He remembered when we were snowed in.

I squirmed and his lips quirked.

While I wanted more than anything to have Silas lick my pussy, I had so many questions. I wasn't as desperate for him as I was last night. Okay, I was, but it could wait. While sex with Silas seemed to be the one thing we had no issues with, I had to make things right. About everything else.

I pushed up, put the coffee on the bedside table next to the clock and took his hand. "I'm sorry, Silas. About everything."

He looked at the floor as if the wood planks fascinated him. "Eve, you don't–"

I gave his fingers a squeeze and he looked at me. The room was dimly lit, but I could see him clearly.

"I do. In your office, I freaked. Completely and totally lost it. I thought you were taking control. You said *we* all the time and I've never been part of a *we* before."

"Me neither," he admitted. "I'm so fucking proud of you, kitten. Your business. How you got the contract for the inn. For running it your way. For the fucking pink t-shirts."

"I... I–"

"You never heard that, did you? That someone's proud of you."

I shook my head and tried not to cry.

"I want you to succeed. To have Steaming Hotties turn into a phenomenon."

"Phenomenon?" I scoffed. "That may be a little far reaching."

I shook my head. "I know a good business when I see

one. I wanted to help you. I envision you supplying coffee to all of the James Inn sites. Hell, to all the James Hotels."

"That's a lot of coffee and world-class nepotism."

He shook his head. "You're my wife. It's my job to give you everything your heart desires."

I couldn't stay still any longer. I climbed from beneath the covers and crawled over to him, wrapped my arms around him from behind.

He laughed as he tried not to slosh the coffee over the brim of his mug. Reaching forward, he set his drink next to mine, then turned so I was in his arms. In his lap.

"How did you get Hyport to sign?" I asked. "I mean, I saw the text you sent Mav, that the deal was dead."

"Hyport heard us. In my office. All of it."

I gasped, tried to squirm away.

"No. It's okay. He... he made me see that I was so driven to buy his business because of my issues with my father. To prove I'm not like him."

"You're not," I told him, taking his face in my hands and making him look at me as I said it. "Even though you got caught watching cam porn that featured your wife."

He smiled. "I know. I do, now. Finally. I think Hyport is more a father to me than mine ever was. No, I know he is."

I could only nod.

"He told me he was proud of me, just like I'm proud of you."

I closed my eyes, kissed his forehead. "We're so much alike."

"What? Stubborn? Mule-headed? Blind?"

I shook my head. "We want what's best for those we love."

He kissed me. So soft. So gentle.

"That's all I wanted for you. The best. I got the plumber to fix your sink because it was a problem I could solve for you."

I laughed.

"And you offered up your trust fund to help close the deal."

I glanced away, then wasn't shamed by it. "I needed them to know you aren't your dad. That if a little more money would sway them, that they could have whatever I could give."

"You've been after that money from the beginning."

I nodded. "Because I didn't have control of it. All I wanted was for it to be mine and mine alone. See? We're totally alike."

"So now what?"

"The deal is done? You now own the Hyport Hotel chain?"

"We do," he clarified.

"I don't want it."

"Well, I don't want Steaming Hotties. I have no clue how to make a good cup of coffee."

I grinned. He was right.

"The first time I saw you," I admitted. "You were making a coffee."

He brushed my hair back from my face, frowned. "It was tequila at the bar."

"Nope. It was right here. Like this. Early in the morning. You, naked."

He shook his head. "I sure as hell would've remembered seeing you, kitten."

I climbed from his lap and grabbed one of his shirts that had been carelessly tossed over a chair in the corner.

"What are you doing?"

"I have to go." I walked out of the bedroom.

"Go?" he asked, following me.

I nodded, gave him a smile as I found a pair of his winter boots by the front door.

"I won't be long."

"Dressed like that? There's tons of snow out there!" I had on his dress shirt and oversized snow boots. And nothing else. From the hook on the wall, I grabbed his winter coat which fell thick and heavy to below my knees.

"I'll call you."

He ran a hand over my neck, probably debating

whether to let me go or tie me up. "Call me? Why are you leaving?"

"Just give me five minutes and it'll make sense. I promise."

He didn't look like I was ever going to make sense.

I cut through the house and went out the back door. The one that was all glass.

"Eve!" he yelled, confused.

I grinned as I trudged through the snow toward my house. To finally, completely, make him mine.

60

SILAS

WHERE THE FUCK was she going? It was freezing. Early. She was practically naked beneath my coat and there was snow. So much snow.

I shut the door and stared into the inky darkness for a moment, then ran to my room to throw clothes on and chase after her.

She hadn't seemed upset. She wasn't freaking out. She smiled. Then why would she leave? Where the *hell* did she go? Wait five minutes? No fucking way.

Before I could tug on boxers, my cell rang.

"Where the hell are you?" I asked, freaking out.

"Go to your back door."

"What?" Had she lost her mind?

"Just do it."

I kept my phone to my ear as I did as she wanted.

"There. That's where I first saw you. Just like that."

"What? Naked in my house?"

"Yes."

"You were making coffee and talking to someone, just like you are now."

I ran a hand over the back of my neck. "What the hell are you talking about?"

"Turn out the light."

"Will it get you back here faster?"

"Yes."

She was crazy. Completely crazy. I did as she said, swiping at the switch on the wall.

"Now look out the back door."

"Eve, I love you, but I think you—"

And there she was. In the house behind me. Naked. I could only see half of her with the window only exposing her from the navel up, but it was her. I knew those gorgeous breasts anywhere.

"What the fuck?" I muttered. "What the hell are you doing in the neighbor's house?"

"I'm your neighbor. This is my house. This is my bedroom window."

I blinked, frozen in the doorway. Staring at my wife, who, it turned out, lived behind me.

"My alarm goes off at five. It never used to be exciting, such an early wake up, until my new naked neighbor moved in. Until every morning, he'd walk around making coffee and talking on the phone."

Holy shit. I never really thought about anyone seeing me. My apartment in Denver was twenty floors up.

"You saw me?"

"You're a billionaire but won't pay for blinds. My win. I saw every inch. Although it's too far away to see the mole on your ass. Let me check again."

I smiled and flipped on the light switch. I could still see her and now she could see me as well. Naked. And hard. For her.

"You watched me," I said.

"Just like you watched me in the cam room."

"That's why you looked so surprised when you first saw me at the bar."

"Yeah. I recognized you, even in clothes." She paused. "Silas, I've always wanted you, from the first time I laid eyes on you. When I didn't know you as more than my new naked neighbor."

"Fuck, kitten. I always wanted you, too."

"Good. Never forget it's your fault, this view I have right now, that made me want you for your dick."

I glanced down at how fucking hard I was for her. I laughed, then laughed some more.

"Get your ass back over here, kitten, and you can have all the dick you want."

"Always?"

"Always."

EPILOGUE

DANIEL

USING MY SHOULDER, I pushed through the door and into the office, my hands full.

"You love gossip, Ang," I said. "News at Steaming Hotties is that the Hunters–not the owner of the mountain, but the other ones–filed for bankruptcy, their house was repossessed by the bank and they relocated during the night to Florida for the guy to take a job at a golf course."

I set the office manager's coffee on her desk.

She eyed me, listening to my words, but not with the usual glee for small town tea spilling. I didn't give a shit about the crazy antics of others, but I figured for once, I could get the edge on her with some juicy info.

"Gambling. Can you believe it?" I added.

She humphed. "There's other ways to gamble," she muttered and I frowned.

Usually, she was as fiery as her red hair and always knew the local news before me.

"What? Did I ruin it for you?" I asked, taking a sip of my black coffee.

"I think you ruined it for yourself."

"What the hell does that mean? I don't even know the Hunters. I know Eve, of course." I raised my to-go cup with the Steaming Hotties logo on the side. "And that's not the exciting part. I guess Eve's ex is going to jail."

I waited for Ang to react, but she didn't. "What's up with you this morning?"

Her eyes widened behind her reading glasses. "Me? I think you have more important things to worry about than other people's problems."

Frowning, I set my cup down, put my hands on her desk and leaned in. "What's going on?" I asked. "No one's hurt?"

Running a tree service company, I always worried about my employees. Chain saws, falling timber and other hazards meant the possibility of bad injuries. That was from working on the trees, not from falling ones. Like the one that we cut up that had fallen through Lindy Beckett's house last summer. Fortunately, no one had been home when her neighbor had played lumberjack.

"No. No one's hurt."

I sighed because it was always in the back of my mind. "Then what's curdled your milk?"

She picked up pink message slips and pushed them into my face.

I snagged them and stepped back.

"I thought you learned your lesson right after high school, Daniel Case Pearson. I mean, I thought out of everyone, you'd know about condoms. Talk about gambling. Getting a girl pregnant? Now? You're forty years old."

I blinked, looked more closely at what Ang wrote. Condoms? Pregnant? What the hell was she talking about?

THE TEST CAME BACK POSITIVE. *You need to call me.*

I TOLD *you this would happen, but no. You thought a little fun wouldn't have consequences. Call me.*

WHERE ARE YOU? *What am I supposed to do, take care of this on my own?*

. . .

FINE, fun was had. Now we face the consequences.

I LIFTED MY HEAD, met Ang's wise, pointed gaze.

"These were on the business voicemail?"

Ang nodded. "I copied those down from the weekend. Exactly as recorded."

"And you think this was me?" I waved the papers. "Chad's a little careless from what I've heard."

"She calls you out by name."

"Who?" I glanced again at the messages. "Who is saying I... I–"

"Got her pregnant?"

I swallowed hard. Nodded.

"Melanie Harwood."

Frowning, I looked to Ang. "Who?"

She shook her head and tsked me like a scolding mother. Since she was close friends with mine, they'd had practice for the past four decades.

"Little Melly Harwood. The librarian. And someone so young, too."

"Young?"

"She can't be more than twenty-four. Mabel's daughter was two years ahead of her in school."

Figuring out how Mabel's daughter had any relevance wasn't important. I didn't know who she was either.

Crushing the papers in my hand, I crossed my arms over my chest. "You think I got a twenty-four year old librarian pregnant?"

"The messages were all directed to you. Remember, you wanted to *get back out there*." She made stupid air quotes with her fingers about how everyone in the office thought I should find a woman.

"Fuck me," I muttered. I ran a hand down my face, stomped into my office and slammed the door shut.

This was a fucking mess.

Dropping into my desk chair, I swiveled back and forth.

What the hell?

I didn't have sex with little Melly Harwood. I didn't even know who she was.

The only sex I'd had recently was with my hand and I wasn't going to share that gem with Ang. My dick and where I put it wasn't any of her business.

But now it was because she took a long line of messages that made it pretty fucking clear I stuck it in the librarian.

I popped to my feet, grabbed my coffee and stormed out of my office.

"Where are you going?" Ang called as I cut past her desk.

"The library."

———

The four James brothers aren't the only alpha males in Hunter Valley. Meet Daniel Pearson, owner of Pearson Tree Service.

Continue on in the On A Manhunt series with Man Scape.

BONUS CONTENT

Guess what? I've got some bonus content for you! Sign up for my mailing list. There will be special bonus content for some of my books, just for my subscribers. Signing up will let you hear about my next release as soon as it is out, too (and you get a free book...wow!)

As always...thanks for loving my books and the wild ride!

Vanessa

JOIN THE WAGON TRAIN!

If you're on Facebook, please join my closed group, the Wagon Train! Don't miss out on the giveaways and hot cowboys!

https://www.facebook.com/groups/
vanessavalewagontrain/

GET A FREE BOOK!

Join my mailing list to be the first to know of new releases, free books, special prices and other author giveaways.

http://freeromanceread.com

ALSO BY VANESSA VALE

For the most up-to-date listing of my books:

vanessavalebooks.com

On A Manhunt

Man Hunt

Man Candy

Man Cave

Man Splain

Man Scape

The Billion Heirs

Scarred

Flawed

Broken

Alpha Mountain

Hero

Rebel

Warrior

Billionaire Ranch

North

South

East

West

Bachelor Auction

Teach Me The Ropes

Hand Me The Reins

Back In The Saddle

Wolf Ranch

Rough

Wild

Feral

Savage

Fierce

Ruthless

Two Marks

Untamed

Tempted

Desired

Enticed

More Than A Cowboy

Strong & Steady

Rough & Ready

Wild Mountain Men

Mountain Darkness

Mountain Delights

Mountain Desire

Mountain Danger

Grade-A Beefcakes

Sir Loin of Beef

T-Bone

Tri-Tip

Porterhouse

Skirt Steak

Small Town Romance

Montana Fire

Montana Ice

Montana Heat

Montana Wild

Montana Mine

Steele Ranch

Spurred

Wrangled

Tangled

Hitched

Lassoed

Bridgewater County

Ride Me Dirty

Claim Me Hard

Take Me Fast

Hold Me Close

Make Me Yours

Kiss Me Crazy

Mail Order Bride of Slate Springs

A Wanton Woman

A Wild Woman

A Wicked Woman

Bridgewater Ménage

Their Runaway Bride

Their Kidnapped Bride

Their Wayward Bride

Relentless

All Mine & Mine To Take

Bride Pact

Rough Love

Twice As Delicious

Flirting With The Law

Mistletoe Marriage

Man Candy - A Coloring Book

ABOUT VANESSA VALE

A USA Today bestseller, Vanessa Vale writes tempting romance with unapologetic bad boys who don't just fall in love, they fall hard. Her books have sold over one million copies. She lives in the American West where she's always finding inspiration for her next story. While she's not as skilled at social media as her kids, she loves to interact with readers.

vanessavaleauthor.com

facebook.com/vanessavaleauthor

instagram.com/vanessa_vale_author

amazon.com/author/vanessavale

bookbub.com/profile/vanessa-vale

tiktok.com/@vanessavaleauthor

Printed in Great Britain
by Amazon